Southside Story

I0553572

Mark Lee

National Library of Canada Cataloging in Publication

Lee, Mark

Southside Story

ISBN 978-0-9867253-1-9

1. Period fiction. 2. Jamaica - Fiction. 3. Caribbean - Fiction

Book design by Abeng Press

Cover design by Beresford Nicholson

Published in Canada by

Abeng Press

DEDICATION

This book is livicated to Grandmamaa and Grandfather, Hilda and Dermot Jones, and Brother Sydney Rickets.

CONTENTS

ACKNOWLEDGMENTS

To the people who lived the trying times, no thanks can repay what you lost or did not achieve. Still, thanks for being. To the singers and players of instruments, keep recording and inspiring thought and courage. Thanks to Renee who typed the first handwritten draft—on a typewriter. To Mike Morrisey who, while taking the manuscript to Jamaica for me from Barbados, shared it with his University of the West Indies colleague and poet, Mervyn Morris, who Mike reported said to get it out right away, 'don't wait on any foreign publishers,' or words to that effect. Thanks Mike and Mervyn. And to the Source of life that makes all things possible...

1 PROLOGUE

Drinking her water
Fuels his fire.

Driftwood, he,
moored alongside a barrier reef
needs to be anchored
deep in her cavern

Earthtremors
He reverberates
exploring the geology of an island
and feels her
volcano erupt.

She pledged to kill him. He had shamed her.
He had dishonoured her womanhood. He had
defiled her temple as a Rastafari daughter. Six
months she nursed her hurt. She cut her two
foot long dreadlocks and burned them in a bin
at the back of her parents' house. It was like a

sacrifice; a private ceremony at which she swore revenge.

"Jah know I going kill you Clavel Smith," she mumbled watching twelve years of knotty dreads shrinking in flames and going up in smoke.

There was a time, in the early days, when her locks had stood for defiance: the rebelliousness of youth against society and family. She wore them openly, dropping over her forehead, about her ears and brushing her shoulder. Then they became vanity: the beauty of woman; the longing for the African woman in bondage to grow tresses as long as European and Asian women. Long hair, which seemed to fascinate the captive African man who despised the stubbly kinks. Sometimes the locks were fully covered, other times they were tied with a scarf about her head and left to flow over her back like a lion's mane.

And when a fuller understanding of Jah, Rastafari had been revealed to Yvonne, the locks came to embody holiness itself: something only her 'King man' should see in the frolicking of their holy lovemaking: dreadlocks that came to represent the sign of the separation of the chosen from the children of Babylon; dreadlocks, that physical other you (I) that always held the personality erect and said "We (I an' I) are not of this world." Never to forget that you are a chosen of Jah. Yvonne's purification.

It was a revelation she had shared only with her King man Jerry and then in a reasoning with her key sistren K.

When Mr and Mrs Stanley drove home from work they were surprised to see their daughter without locks. Mrs Stanley said, "Oh Yvonne, I almost didn't recognise you." Yvonne, who was sitting on the veranda, made a sound of acknowledgement of their presence.

"Now you look like my daughter again," Mrs Stanley said. "What caused this sudden change?"

"Mama, Ah really don't want to talk about it," Yvonne scowled.

"Everything all right Vonnie?" asked her chocolate coloured father with salt and pepper hair.

"Yes daddy. But as Ah said, Ah don't want to talk about it now." Then after a pause she asked in a more relaxed tone, "Daddy, you know anybody at the embassy? I'd like to go up to New York or Miami for a little while just to cool out."

Mr Stanley owned a reasonably successful hardware store. He had a brother who was a senior civil servant. "That shouldn't be a problem," he said. "Get your documents together. If my contacts can't work, your Uncle Herbert should be able to help you."

When the Stanleys were alone in their bedroom changing into home wear Mrs Stanley said, "Ken, I'm sure it had something to do with that...that Clavel she's been seeing. I don't trust him. I've never liked him from the start. Jerry was bad enough but at least he was from a good background. This...this fellow, he seems so...so criminal."

"Now dear, this might just be your prejudice

against the Rastas and the locks and all that. Anyway, he hasn't been around for some time now," he said.

"Ken, Jerry was a Rasta too and that I didn't like but he was a nice person. This one..," she made a throaty tone which said "no good". Mr Stanley agreed that the man did look aggressive and a bit anti social.

Mr Stanley returned to the veranda and sat in a chair beside Yvonne. He had the afternoon's edition of the STAR with the headline: GUNMEN ROB BANK OF $1/2 MILLION. As he glanced at the paper Yvonne said, "Daddy, I'm going to take your advice and send Tafari to boarding school." Tafari was her eleven year old son.

Yvonne got the visa a few weeks later. She booked her passage for a Sunday. On the Saturday night before her departure she dressed like a disco queen. Unbeknownst to him, she borrowed her father's semiautomatic pistol which he kept in a nightstand beside his bed, stuffed the gun into her handbag and drove her Volkswagen Bug to Le Club, a trendy disco at the top of a towering building in New Kingston.

The room was crowded with beautiful women and elegant men milling in the semi dark. A heavy reggae beat pounded from the resident disc jockey; a group with wine glasses stood watching the dancers on the floor under which lights flickered. Cigarette smoke hung in the air conditioned atmosphere. Yvonne walked over to the square sunken bar at the centre of the room and angled her body between two patrons on tall stools.

In the changing multi coloured lights she looked bewitchingly beautiful with weaved on braids and dressed in a glistening halter midi dress.

"Can I help you ma'am?" a barman asked respectfully.

"A double screwdriver," she said coolly. She found a seat in a dark corner, had her drink and left the disco.

Back on the boulevard of tall buildings a cabbie probed, "Taxi ma'am?" When he heard the ghetto destination he hesitated about taking the job but he was reassured by her good looks and dress.

2 CARIBBEAN BLUES

Many people ask
Why don't Caribbean artists paint
pictures of green and shades
of green. The scene
spread with sunshine yellow
One in which leaves mellow
becoming brown, matching
ground, with trees by silver waters
rolling over ashen pebbles;
such scenes are fine
But
we also have Caribbean blues
that bathe souls
of Blacks blending with shadows
and sidewalk greys; flowing reds
from busted heads.
Silvers: beaded drops of sweat
on days when yellow sun is fire
and green is temptation

for hungry bellies.

The sun shone brilliantly but was not hot. When the wind whipped across the parade ground it sent an icy chill through your soul. But the sixty recruits did not flinch. Even their uniforms seemed obedient: they did not move unlike the tall green pine and mahogany forest which imprisoned the mountain camp.

"Companee preseeent arms!!!" The bark from the commanding officer carried up the slope to the corridors of the overhanging officers and Headquarters building which were the pavilions for this passing out parade. In this clean, crisp air the crack of the officer's command carried for miles. Maybe it was the forest and the buzz of traffic on the distant plains that prevented the city of Kingston from hearing the order.

But only one sound answered: the lightning crack of sixty men, each lifting his right arm, slapping the rifle on his left shoulder and bringing the gun pointing upward, in both hands, dead centre before him. To the ear only one man moved. To the eye a machine with red top and black bottom performed one of its motions.

The friends and families in the gallery applauded the new soldiers in red tunics and black pants. The men were frozen again like mannequins on display.

That was two years ago for Clavel Smith, private in the 2nd Battalion of the National

Regiment. He was alert tonight as he drove the Captain in the short wheel base Land Rover. The men called Smith "Reds" because of his rusty complexion and because they said he thought like a Russian. In a classroom session during training at New Castle an instructor had asked, "What would you do if, while on sentry duty one night, you saw suspicious movements within your range, Smith?!" "Shoot to kill, Sah!" came the immediate response. Others in the class had said they would fire to scare.

The convoy of army vehicles moved steadily down the wide street. Hardly anything else drove by at that time of night except those scurrying from parties and night spots. The buildings along the street were in darkness. Captain Bogle sat relaxed in the passenger seat. His light brown skin qualified him as white anywhere in the Caribbean. He had a confident manner and indifferent attitude. Combined with his stern, chiselled features which displayed no emotion, he seemed to Clavel like a man to be obeyed. In societies where colour and economic lines run concurrently and white beggars are never seen, such perceptions are acquired.

"Where are you from Smith?" the captain asked.

"Manchester, SIR."

"You came to the army straight from the country?"

"No, SIR." Smith volunteered nothing.

"So you lived in Kingston for long?"

"Six months, SIR."

"Why did you choose the army?"

"Since Ah was in school, Ah always want to be a soljer, SIR."

Captain Bogle was as bored with the conversation as Smith was uncomfortable with the interrogation. The officer hushed. Under the amber light of the sodium vapour lamps the convoy continued. The night breeze from the sea ahead whipped Smith's face.... Was this as cool as Medina, the tiny village in the May Day Mountains of Manchester? No.

...When mi used to wake up early morning, before the sun come up, dat neva cool, dat was cold. An' de dew pon de grass bwoy...When mi lead de goat down to Mass' Lloyd pasture, mi woulda wash mi face wid de dew. Sista Nelson used to tell we dat de dew keep yu skin young. When she dead and dem bring her body back to her house she did really look young in de casket. An' de coldsweat pon her face, mi neva know it was de ice; me t'ink it was dew water. She was really a nice lady. If wasn't she an' Mass' Lloyd a lot of time mi wouldn't go to school, or eat dinner. Mass' Lloyd always trust mama t'ings out 'im grocery shop even though im know t'ings tough; an' Sista Nellie, anytime she go Mandeville she come up to de house: "Sista B, see if this shirt can fit the little man." An' is Mass' Lloyd who sign mi papers fo mi to join the army.....

As the convoy approached the wide intersection at Victoria Avenue and South Camp Road, the radar controlled traffic lights flicked to green.

"Straight ahead Smith," Captain Bogle said,

"We're going to assist the police in an operation in Southside. Too many gunshots are being fired in this city."

"Yes sir."

3 HOUSE HUNTIN

Johnny and Valerie livin'
in Jones Town
and as poor people
one Sunday when she tendin' de yout'
an cookin'
him huntin' roomin'
For hours him walkin' in de sun
dat not shinin' like how it burnin'
Sidewalk hot, shoes dunnin', no bus fare
an' him fearin'
dat street work crashin'
(It shouldn't, for garbage pilin', stinkin')

Ah!...
Johnny smilin' for de sky
cloudin' and him tinkin' is shadin
but now, Oh raah!! It rainin'
him wettin', soakin
so him beggin' shelterin'

Over de patterin' pourin'
him could barely hear
de fellow on de veranda shoutin'
Sorry, can't help yu!
Ah packin', movin'
Land lord sayin' no children
playin' an' my Queenie breedin.

"Mama, when me grow big, yu nuh, I goin' just get my Magnum an' shoot off all dem Babylon..."

"No Tafari, you mustn't talk like that," Yvonne said.

They were in their two room wooden shack. It was one of four or five barracks like coops at the back of the yard set away from the main decayed house of crumbling red bricks. The shacks formed an L with the back fence of corrugated metal sheets. There was a gate which exited into a narrow asphalt paved alley, Water Lane. In the old days when Rae Town and Breezy Castle were top residential areas of Kingston, the lane and the back entrance were for services. The maid and yard boy used it; the bread , milk and postmen used it; and refuse for the garbage men was emptied at the back gate.

The outer buildings, the shacks, were for the servants. The kitchen linked the main house and the shacks. The main house was a two storey family structure with four bedrooms, living and dining areas, a study, a patio upstairs and a veranda downstairs. Each room was now a flat occupied by a family. A bathroom and a toilet, which were used by everyone who lived there and their visitors, were in the row with the shacks and the kitchen, also used by everyone who lived in the yard.

The ground skirting the house was paved. A walkway about 25 feet long, of cracked and broken black and white marble tiles, stretched from the front of the house to a fancy patterned green wrought iron gate exiting to the wide street. There was another wider double gate at another end of the low brick and wrought iron fence, for carriages or cars in the old days, which swung open over bare pale brown earth.

Like the similar neighbouring yards, forty people lived and fought and hated and loved here. When Yvonne and Jerry first moved here, Mr Hudson, the little old man who sat all day in Miss Dorothy's grocery and snackette across the lane, would tell Yvonne how she was living in a grand house.

"The Benjamins used to live there," he would say in a proud manner to show that he knew an influential family from a long time ago. "The one who is the High Court judge now, the young one, he used to be very sickly as a child and his father had to be waking up my uncle at all hours of the night to avoid going out to Public Hospital. My uncle was a dispenser, you know. Boy would wake up screaming in the dead of night. Couple o' times they prepared the buggy and pull out but by the time they get to East Queen Street, boy quiet as a lamb and then burst out laughing. Just wanted fresh air you know. Nineteen ought seven earthquake didn't budge that house.

"Old man Benjamin built on and sold off some of the land after the nineteen ought seven earthquake fire. He died right there you know, in '52 or '53, can't remember but it was after hurricane Charlie in '51. The wife died a few years earlier and the boys were back from school in England quite a few years and moved up to St Andrew's. The boys were stand offish and didn't like when black people started moving into the area. Can't say a blame them for look what the area come to with the guns and the ganja and the politics... But the daddy, he knew where he had made his wealth. Is the poor country people who came to the haberdashery in Princess Street... Townsend, the undertaker chap, he bought out from the boys about '55..," and he would go on and on.

Things had changed by 1976. Most of the shingles on the roof were replaced by corrugated sheets in the '60s. The red bricks were painted over in loud colours and the outhouses were more termite, cockroach and newspaper than wood and corrugated iron.

"But mama, the Babylon shoot Daddy Jerry and he never did anything wrong. And all the boys at school boast about their daddy and I don't have any daddy."

Yvonne looked compassionately at her son. He sat squashed into the dining table because the make shift clothes closet behind did not allow the chair to be properly pulled out. She sat on the edge of the bed which ran parallel to the table with a passage with barely enough room for one person. She held her

Nefertitarian, regal pose as Tafari put the last bit of fried fish and johnny cake to his mouth.

"Tafari, Daddy Jerry would not like you to talk like that. You remember how he always teach you the song 'Peace and Love'?"

"Yes mama."

"Well that is a Rastafari chant that the brethren would sing at Nyabinghi. And you know how important 'Binghi is to Daddy Jerry and the brethren, right?" He nodded. "Peace and love is just as important to I and I the Rastafari as 'Binghi and the dreadlocks that we wear, seen?" she ended questioningly.

"Yes mama."

She was thinking, "Ah wonder if he really understand. He looks so much like his father. Ah wonder if he will have Jerry's understanding." She said, "Is because of the love that we have for Jah and you that we name you Tafari, for that was the name of the King before he was crowned Emperor Haile Selassie I, seen?"

"Yes mama."

"And when you hear them talking about their father, just remember that your father is the King of kings, right? O.K., go and brush your teeth now and Ah walk with you out to Tower Street."

"Cho man, mama, I am eight now yu nuh, and when I reach to Tower Street and South Camp Road I can cross the street by myself."

She got the message. He didn't want the other children to feel he was any "likkle sissy bwoy". As he left she thought how he had the looks and the pride of Jerry...

...They had met in 1967. She was in the fifth form at Homestead High, a school for girls founded by the Church of England in Jamaica. He was in his first year at the Mona campus of the University of the West Indies. He hadn't seen her in her green and white plaid tunic which identified her as a schoolgirl. But as a university man he'd probably still have been attracted to the girl who carried the countenance of the Egyptian Queen Nefertiti.

It was a Saturday when she was headed for the Old Dramatic Arts Theatre at one end of the campus, for extra 'O' level examination classes run by the Guild of Undergraduates. He was going in the opposite direction to the Faculty of Social Sciences to make stencilled copies of a flier. It was to publicise a 'Grounation' with Dr Walter Rodney, Guyanese historian, lecturer and idol to undergrads and some faculty who identified with the African liberation struggle.

Jerry's and Yvonne's paths crossed, literally, because the trodden footpath she walked cut diagonally across the tiled walkway he was on, which together formed a massive X across the manicured campus greens.

"What have we here, a dignified African princess?" the lanky Jerry began. She smiled a shy smile. "It appears most appropriate that you should be the first one to be invited to a Grounation with Brother Walter Rodney next week Sunday in the Students' Union," he charmed.

"Don't know if I can come," she replied as he changed course to stride eagerly alongside her. His floral dashiki, faded blue jeans, brown leather sandals, red, green and black "liberation" wrist band, semi combed hair and brown cardboard folder said 'campus man'.

"Do you live on hall?"

"I'm not a student here."

"O.K. Lecturer's daughter. You can still come."

"Sorry, Homestead fifth former going to extra lessons," she said thinking, "That going turn him off."

But if he was disappointed or shocked it didn't show. He just said, "Sunday, 4 o'clock at Students' Union. Music, poetry, refreshment and there won't be any charge. I'm going to run off some fliers now so I'll drop some off by Old Dramatic Arts after your class."

He kept his promise and they exchanged names. She went to the Grounation with two friends from Homestead who were also interested in Black Power. They told their parents they were going to the zoo at the Hope Botanical Gardens near the campus.

During the function, Yvonne surprised herself by getting up and speaking out against the "system". Maybe it was the oratory of Rodney, the poetry of Bongo Ever or the pounding heartbeat rhythm of the Mystic Revelation of Rastafari band that moved her emotions. And when the sixteen year old schoolgirl shrilled, "We can't sit down here in Jamaica and Guyana and Trinidad and Barbados or wherever and let it become like

Rhodesia or South Africa brothers and sisters," and the crowd roared and the bass drum echoed them, her spirit soared.

After that she and Jerry got close. He pretending that it was a solely 'conscious' relationship, she playing the game while, out of an unspoken loyalty to Jerry, resisting the swoops of the other hawkish conscious brethren who did not conceal that they wanted her body.

He introduced her to an organisation called the Revolutionary African Solidarity (RAS), a group of high school students led by a young lawyer president with whom they met on Monday afternoons. The lawyer who gave himself an African name by deed poll taught them that certain words they used in the local vernacular like 'chacka chacka' (untidy), 'nyam' (eat) and 'unno' (you collective) were actually genuine Yoruba or Twi words and not bad English as they were told at home and in school; that saying 'the boy dem' instead of 'the boys' was exactly the way words were pluralized in some African languages: by adding 'them'.

Things happened fast in those days. That summer she was out of school with three of the eight 'O' level subjects she sat. Her mother identified Jerry as the reason for Yvonne's dismal results. "He's always here with this nonsense about Black Power and Africa. We're not Africans, we're Jamaicans. I agree we're descended from Africans but we are mixed. All of us in Jamaica are mixed. Even your good Jerry. Even though he's dark skinned, look at the quality of his hair. Which African has that good quality hair? He has some Indian or Chinese or something."

"Mummy his grandfather, Dr Henry, might have some white ancestry...but mummy, if you had a dollar, seventy five cents in copper and 25 cents silver, and you were forced with having to give up one set, which would you cling to? Jerry is holding on to his seventy five per cent African."

Jerry dropped out of university after the riots in 1968 when the police teargassed demonstrators protesting against the government's deportation of Walter Rodney and two other Caribbean political activists. He said it was in solidarity with the brothers. It was also to seek a job to support the pregnant Yvonne.

It was tough. He had drifted from the political aspect of the struggle towards the religious. Being a humanist, Jerry was disillusioned with socialism and the thought of killing people for the revolution. He started growing dreadlocks and where his 'A' levels and year and odd at university qualified him for a job, his hair and Rasta lingo disqualified him.

The daily newspaper agreed to take freelance contributions from him but they wouldn't send a Rasta on assignment in Jamaica 1968. The Stanleys said Yvonne had to leave the home in the middle class neighbourhood of Vineyard Town where there were still lawns and gardens even though upper St Andrew addresses had now become the vogue.

Jerry did not want to impose on his grandfather who reared him and a space writer's stipend could not take a backroom in Vineyard Town. They could not find one in Rollington Town or Franklyn Town just down the actual and social road.

One of the Rasta brethren who travelled with the Mystic Revelations band provided a temporary answer. During a visit to his 'gates' as he called his shanty on the Wareika Hills to the east of Kingston, on hearing of their plight Ras Breeze said, "But Brother Jerry, de I could just control a spot 'pon de hillside man. Yes I. I an' I will help de I construct a gates I ah. For sooner than later de I an' de daughter have to step from out o' Babylon."

The thought of living in Wareika Hills in a bamboo and zinc sheet shanty shook Yvonne inside. What would her parents think? Wareika, the haunt of gunmen, thieves and Ras... "I am one now anyway and who put me out of whose house?" she thought.

"Give Jah thanks we never lived there more than six months and when Tafari born we came straight to Water Lane from the hospital," Yvonne thought.

Pow pow pow pow!!! a pistol barked.

Rat atat a tat!!! an M 16 rifle responded.

It awoke Yvonne from her reverie. "Jesus Christ...Tafari!" she cried as she jumped from the bed towards the door. But he was safe. He was on the other side of South Camp Road now where Rae Town, unlike Southside was not under police military curfew.

4 FICTION...

...nothing but imagination
de experts
watch dem machinations
Take Tommy,
dem say him is
a test tube baby
Travel on a tube
wit' him London sounds
supersonic touch down inna Kingston town
Him high tech brain
on England not a drain
like him bridge dat never know
de Portland rain.
All Mass Arthur crops wash 'way
an' that was just because
"Tommy boob tube SAY"
that life is FICTION

People sufferation

Tommy computer malfunction.
News media explanation.

Now we not a machine nation;
more the Third World situation
shanty habitation
high rise rehabilitation
checkin the population
fo' the annual computation.
An' Tommy expire
for the figures never match
Water the dam never catch
No one know whether it was a suicide fire
or burn out
from a short circuit wire...
But this is fiction
Not the story of a nation.

"First trip to Jamaica?"

"Nah. Been down there a coupla times."

"I hear it's quite an experience there with all the shooting and fires..."

"Tell the truth bud, I've seen worse. I usually stay in Negril or Montego Bay and you wouldn't believe it's the same country you hear about in the news in the States. I tell you, I've been to Kingston where most of the action is at and I've seen worse in New York City."

"I'll be based in Kingston... Work for a Canadian company... Got a contract from the Canadian government to install a microwave communications system for the Jamaican government. We did one a few years back for the Cubans. From here we go to Barbados where we'll install some stations for the smaller islands. Hear it's nice and slow out there."

"Yeah. I gotta buddy who flew Nam with me who went down there and set up business...small inter island airline."

"Hey, I did a tour of Nam too... Maybe you could gimme your bud's name and we could do some business out there. We gotta have reliable transport and I hear these islands can be the pits."

Their conversation was interrupted by the stewardess on the PA system. "Ladies and gentlemen we're now descending into Sangster airfield, Montego Bay. Please fasten your seatbelts and bring your chairs to the upright position... Those of you disembarking..."

When the aircraft touched down, Chris Murphy the telecommunications engineer turned to Brad Wisebaum and said "Beautiful landing." The taller Wisebaum who resembled the standard print of Jesus Christ, looked across the engineer through the window and nodded in agreement.

The customs arrival hall sweltered. Most of the passengers had disembarked here but it was not the crowd which caused the heat. In fact it was not much of a crowd. Tourism was not bright this year. The air conditioning system was out. The carousel was immobile. The luggage was slow in arriving and in the big hall, there were no open windows, no fans, no seats. Wisebaum took off his denim jacket and laid it across his knees as he sat on the carousel. He watched the openings through which the luggage would normally enter the hall and occasionally wiped sweat from his brow.

A red haired woman accompanying a blubbery man whose skin showed through his soaked white shirt, turned towards Brad and sneered, "Isn't this ridiculous?!" He half smiled and shrugged and she interpreted it as agreement.

When the luggage was finally hauled in on a wagon, the customs officers did not bother to search the visitors. But they were rigorous with the locals, searching for prohibited items such as apples, grapes and cornflakes. Brad Wisebaum picked up his haversack and canvas duffle bag. He pushed the swinging doors and felt a welcome gust of less fetid air. He sighed inside thinking how easily the two dismantled hand guns in the bag could have been five or six.

He stopped and fitted his shades to cut the glare. The outside sounds rushed at him, minibuses and taxis moving off, red caps and taxi drivers offering their service in pseudo American accents, the muffled public address system telling a departing passenger to accept a call.

"Brad man!" a voice hailed.

The tall man who looked like Christ in jeans and shades spun his head. A grinning Skully, white teeth in a black face came briskly toward him. "Come nuh star, de car over so." He gestured across the parking lot which was covered with cars and dotted with almond trees. "De man had a good flight?"

"Yeah mon. Everything irie. Everything cool." Pseudo Rastafarian reply.

The very black Skully bobbed and weaved the way to the car. "Straight to Negril, or we brakes in the Bay a while?"

"Let's have a beer at the 'Mango Tree' before we go mon."

Wisebaum sat in the rear of the '71 Buick taxi and Skully pulled it out of the parking lot. He swung up the sloped road towards the green hills dotted with white mansions that formed one backdrop to Montego Bay. They continued up what is popularly called Top Road, where, when you looked over to the right it was as though you were in an aeroplane again: the low lying terminal buildings, the control tower, the 727 and DC10 aircraft, the lagoon and the blue Caribbean sea rolled below.

They were soon at the crest of the rise heading to town with its low buildings and then they were pulling up outside the Mango Tree.

This semi thatched cafe representing, presumably, 'native' life in a transistorised metropolis was always busy. It attracted locals and visitors alike of all classes. To some extent tourism and carnivals have that in common: people trade in their egos for a period of fun.

Brad and Skully took a table midway between the circular bar and the entrance. The bar was covered. Where they sat was open. A beautiful chocolate coloured girl who smelled of cheap perfume came over and took their order. Two beers; one hot, one cold.

"Mon, how do you guys drink warm beer,"

Brad said, "must taste like piss."

"Move de gas off yu chest," Skully said and belched.

"So what's been happening Skull?"

"Bwoy, security all over de place. Just last week soljer and police raid a coolie man over Petersfield, move with about a hundredweight of cured collie, level a field and carry 'way 'bout ten grand US cash. Yu know is soljer hustling that; herb, money an' all."

"So what's new?" Brad jibed. He was serious too about the seeming security omnipresence, because that was why they drove as they did. A black man driving a white tourist in the front seat of a taxi attracted attention at police roadblocks. "What's with the girls mon; you get that chick from Sav pregnant yet?"

"You go on man, you is a joker. Talkin' 'bout baby, you bring de feeding fo' me sah? Can't get nothing like dat in shops 'bout here. Only milk powder an' cornmeal; dat dem want we feed the youth dem; and de communis' condensed milk from Cuba."

"I thought you said Rasta didn't deal with politricks? Anyway, you're a bald head Rasta," Brad joked. "Yeah, I brought formula for two babies because I know that girl in Sav is gonna make you a father again mon."

When the Buick drove past West Gate Shopping Centre, signifying the western limit of the city, Skully surveyed the green canefields on either side of the road and felt relaxed. He pushed a cassette in the car player, fidgeted with the knobs and then the Mighty Diamonds blared:

"Marcus Garvey prophesy say
It a go bitter,
Man a go find themself against the wall.."
"Yu see how things run red now, you don't see nutten yet. Is next year, 77... Marcus say when the two sevens clash a certain politician head going roll and blood going flow down King Street like a river," Skully said over the music.
"But when the right time come
Some a go charge fi murder..."
He craned his neck to look at Brad in the rearview mirror: "Ah have some o' de right stuff for de man," he grinned and as if from nowhere presented a rolled spliff wadded with sinsemilla.

"What have we got here, cannabis sativa," Brad guffawed and lit up with paper match from his pocket.
"But when the right time come
Some a go charge fi arson...
Swallowfield a go be the battlefield...."
They continued westward and the scenery was enough to make you high. The spotless green and blue hills to the left beckoned a welcome. The white sand beaches to the right and the sun invited relaxation and the teasing blue and emerald and every shade between sea called "enter me". Occasionally a little wooden shack appeared along the snaking asphalt road, bedecked with the tropical yellows and oranges and reds and green and purple: ripe bananas, oranges, tangerines, papayas, grapefruit, ackee and star apple. Then a little boy or girl in 'poor me soul' canvas shoes and

tattered clothes would step forward holding up bunches of fruit.

Brad drew on the spliff. When the reggae music thumped, he wondered about the violence of the lyrics and the seduction of the beat: the heartbeat on guitar, "chi chi chi chi", reggae, reggae.

Like the pied piper inviting you into the unknown. And what is the unknown? Death? Must not think this kind of thought. A white man in a black country where the talk is of anti imperialism and back to Africa and freeing South Africa. You can never be too careful.

Must show strength always. But no need to take unnecessary risks like the guys who brought in counterfeit dough. Premature death. Most people think they died when the twin engine Cessna crashed, but everyone in St Ann knows that they landed safely.

They came with more of the duds and Mr Big invited them up to his house like nothing had happened, gave them both samples of the stuff and while they were making up the joints WHAM! Mr Big himself took off one head with a razor sharp machete. 'Blacker' took the other. Their guns and jewellery were taken and the bodies put back in the plane which was pushed over a precipice and then lit.

Mr Big's boys told the police about the plane and the newspaper story said it crash landed and burned. No. I prefer my style. Columbus could still do well here. Guns for Ja dollars. Ja dollars for weed and I'm gone.

"Wha' happen star, de man all right?" Skully interrupted.

"Yeah mon. Cool runnings."

When Chris Murphy disembarked from the plane at Norman Manley International Airport, Kingston, what struck him first was that his flight was the only one in or out...at that moment. There were no other aeroplanes on the tarmac. When he entered the terminal building, the feeling that he was not in an international airport remained. This was just a big open space with a big building at which he had arrived by plane.

When at last he exited the building and walked down the corridor with the low roof supported by iron posts he thought, "Jose Marti International in communist Cuba was more alive than this."

A dozen or so burly black women loitered on concrete seats or stood around. He went towards nowhere, stopped and looked towards anywhere: taxis were there. He was wondering whether Marc Fortesque had forgotten him when a voice beside him asked, "Hi. Any dallars for sale?" He turned. "Pardon?"

"You got any dallars...US...for sale? I'll give you two for one. You only get one sixty in the bank."

Was this a scam. Oh my God where's the police? Marc...

"Well, well Chris Murphy is in town," a voice eased his panic. Marc's voice. "As usual, Chris has made a friend on arrival, et une fille."

Murphy turned to the woman, "Sorry," and stooped for two of his bags. Chris tipped a Red

Cap who had pushed the remaining luggage on a trolley, then they loaded Marc's sleek baby Chev and drove off.

"Can't say I've ever been happier to see you, Marc. That woman..."

"Relax. She meant no harm. She's what the Jamaicans call a higgler. She goes to Panama, Haiti, Cayman, Miami and shops for things like onions, cornflakes, bath soap which are scarce here and sells them at a good, pardon the pun, black market price."

"So this is socialism a la Jamaique?!"

"Call it what you will, it's survival, buddy."

Marc flicked on the radio.

"One man was killed in a joint police and military operation in Southside this morning. Eyewitness reports said the man identified only as Boy Blue was standing at his gate when a joint police and military party accosted him and opened fire.

"The reports say he was still alive when the police put him on the floor of a jeep but that the security forces continued their operations in the area before taking Boy Blue to hospital.

"He was pronounced dead on arrival at the Kingston Public Hospital.

"When our newsroom contacted the Police Media Centre they confirmed that a man was killed during an operation in Central Kingston but said it was in a shoot out with the security forces. They say an official report on the operation will be given later today....

"Meanwhile, in other crime news...Four masked gunmen escaped with over 100,000 dollars following the hold up of the May Pen branch of the Bank of..."

"Christ Jesus, Marc, don't tell me that this is what Canada has sent me to."

"Relax, Uncle Sam sent you to Vietnam, didn't he. You just heard that the police got a gunman, and robbers shook down a bank. One point for good one for evil."

"Lemme tell you what I just heard bud: State execution of a private citizen, government managed news, a bank was robbed probably to fund some terrorists and some big black tub o lard almost mugged me at the airport."

"And remember to watch your language. Jamaicans are very touchy about certain things..." He paused. "Look Chris, things are not always what they seem. A dog's bark is often worse than its bite. Tonight we're taking you to a party. Guys from the political directorate, businessmen, army brass...a good mix will be there and you'll see what I mean.

"I tell you Chris, a man could make it here. We do things for them, they do things for us."

The soldiers and police had established a joint operations base in Southside and from there patrols were dispatched in different sectors. Clavel was in a patrol of three soldiers and a policeman. The soldiers wore battle green fatigues, the police navy blue drill. The soldiers carried M16 rifles, while the police were armed with stubby machine guns.

The patrol had just entered the narrow alley

of clustered houses behind Yvonne's yard when they saw two men approaching. Patrol and men saw each other in the same instant. One of the two men pulled something from his waist and began as if he were throwing something.

Pow pow pow pow!!! At the sound of gunshots the security men flung themselves to the ground. *Rat-a-tat-a-tat!* The gunman was dancing to the tune of Pvt. Clavel Smith's M16. Head almost severed, he twitched and was soon limp and broken on the pavement.

The other man was over the fence into Yvonne's yard in a flash. He climbed the stairs of the main house on to the landing then jumped to the roof of the house next door. There he stopped and took off his shirt and trousers revealing soccer jersey and shorts. He stuffed the garments he'd taken off into a plastic bag and stuck it under the eave, then jumped from the roof. He exited into the lane where a crowd was gathering and and headed towards the scene shouting "Murder! Murder! Me see it. Me see it. De yout' never do nutten an' unno just shoot him!"

Two of the soldiers had gone into Yvonne's yard searching for the man who had fled. They went cautiously, expecting to be fired on as they went from room to room hauling out occupants and poking under beds. They covered the yard from the lane to the front street but the man had vanished. They didn't recognise him in soccer gear.

When they returned to the scene, several patrols had converged there. A V-150 armoured car blocked the lane at the intersection where the patrol had originally entered and a police jeep was there, radio crackling.

The crowd was being whipped up by the young man in football outfit. This was how "dem" treat poor people he was saying. "Yu t'ink dem soljer and police bway could go up St Andrew and do dem kind o' t'ings. Dis have to reach court. Me see everything..."

A woman was saying "Bwoy Blue would neva so fool fool to even walk wit gun an' 'im know say soljer inna de area. We mus' march go de Gleaner an' de radio and TV station, man. We want justice inna de ghetto!"

The security men began ordering the crowd off the street. Clavel was with a group of policemen in a huddle around the corpse. Clavel was sweating. This was the first time he had fired live shots at a man. He had shot to kill. The man was dead.

To kill a man... It felt strange. Not like killing bald pates in Medina with a pebble, wooden rifle powered by a bicycle's or car's rubber tubing. The little boys used to go down to Mass Lloyd's pasture where the mango trees and the pimento berries were reflected in the green pond at which the animals watered. The birds loved it there because of the food and water. They never seemed to fear man...or boy. You'd hear the parakeets making that screechy sound and the doves cooing. The pimento trees perfumed the woods. The cattle fanned flies with their tails, contented.

The sun made patterns through the green leaves onto the fallen musty brown ones. That was where we went to kill birds. It wasn't a place for killing but for living. When the stone hit the bird you felt something thud in you and you knew that all life was connected. When we roasted the bird and ate, that was life. When the bullets hit the man I felt the stabs. Not the same as hitting the bird. You can't eat the man. Murder? No. The law of the forest and the law of this concrete jungle are the same: kill to survive.

****

Boy Blue was a member of one of the gangs that ruled the streets of the ghetto. They were violent, they were vicious. Some most people said they were connected to political parties. They designated certain areas as their own and their party's, giving the turf the names of past or present international battlefields. Dunkirk, Saigon, Tel Aviv. The gangs had names like Vikings and Skull. Their heroes were from comic books, westerns and war movies.

At first there weren't many guns; only stiletto like pen knives known as tooth picks, ratchet released knives and the occasional .22 or .38 revolver stolen from householders.

A gang of these "rude boys" as they were then known, would stop a pedestrian at election time: "Which party yu fo'?" If the victim answered wrong he'd get a "telephone" cut from one ear to his mouth, often exposing teeth. If he answered "None", the gangster would probably remove his shoe and slice his sole with the unfriendly advice, "Join a 'P' man."

The gangs also fought each other with knives, stones, bottles, machetes and guns. The early gangs rode bicycles or "lalas" as they called them and then graduated to small 50 cc motorbikes. The battles were sometimes humorous. Once two Vikings men rode back to back on a bike through enemy territory shooting and being shot at. When the skirmish was over the burly pillion rider spat: a .22 cartridge and a front tooth fell.

Some of the gangs had ranges usually in Wareika Hills where they practised shooting.

There was one 'Kid' (as in Rawhide Kid) who, before the police killed him in a shoot out in West Kingston, could hit a target while doing an aerial somersault. And the gangsters were graded in army ranks from general down. That is how they came to be called 'rankings' or 'top rankin'.

In the gangland community a top rankin' or a 'general' had all power over a 'posse'. He was the link with the invisible decent politician and was usually a 'contractor' responsible for distributing government contracts for such as minor road works particularly near holiday seasons. He was also in charge of the distribution of guns.

Unarmed, he was feared even by 20 underlings armed to the teeth. His rivals would rather sneak up on him in some hopeless position such as when he was making love. Rankings didn't take unnecessary chances and fired their guns fairly accurately.

Boy Blue was still a 'bwoy' in the business.

Once, he and a group held up a printery. With the gun held aloft and in a motion as though he were pelting stones, he fired at the proprietor in his tiny office. One shot did graze the man's forehead and lodged in a wall. But most of the shots ended up in the ceiling since Boy Blue discharged the bullet before pointing the gun. Then the man having regained his composure, calculatedly stuffed his index finger into the nozzle of the .38 revolver.

When Boy Blue squeezed the trigger again the gun shattered in his hand. He ran nursing a sprained wrist and his posseros trailed hot on his heels.

"Onnu must save the gunshots for Ian Smith and them who a keep down Africa and Black progress," Yvonne was saying to the security men, her head craned over the corrugated zinc fence of her yard. "But Marcus say black people won't know themself until them back against the wall." Clavel looked up. "*What such a beautiful, intelligent looking girl doing in this ghetto?*" he wondered. Her hair was wrapped in a floral print fabric and she was beautiful.

Clavel looked away from her and his eyes fell on the old man sitting on the stool in the little shop across the lane. Mr Hudson, grey hair, long sleeved shirt buttoned to the neck looked at Clavel.

The old man's eyes reminded him of an owl that perched motionless in the hollow of a tree by the pond in Medina, only opening and shutting its round mirror eyes. Clavel thought:

What does he know? That I looked at the girl longingly or that I killed the boy?"

Hudson was thinking, "*Man after my own heart. I remember '38 when they called us out of barracks. Some from Fort Rocky, some from Fort Clarence, some from Camp. Stationed us at Central Police Station just up the road there. Phone ring say they want us down at the waterfront. Men making worries for more pay. When we get there, mob swarming up every street and lane from the port. The lorry stop and we jump out and the boots on the ground sound like gunshots. Every man Mark 7 ready. When the mob come up on us we opened fire over their head. Then they backed off.*

"*Bustamante pushing up his chest and talking 'bout 'Leave the people alone. Shoot me instead.' He lucky it wasn't left up to me.*

"*When a man come like that before a soldier he asking for trouble. Like that white colonel at Rocky in '42. He know we at war and people say all kind of German submarine is lurking off the coast. I guarding the camp and he walking 'round in the dark like he making sport. I know is him but I take him on. 'Halt!' I say. He frighten and stop. 'Hands in the air.' He obey. 'Advance and be identified!' He come up looking shakey shakey. 'Very Good gunner Hudson,' he said. 'But what would you have done if I had not obeyed?' I lowered the Mark 7, came to the 'shun, saluted and said, 'Fire to kill SAH!' After that, any night he coming out to check, he start whistling from way out and slapping his cane against his trousers. Sometimes you have to put a man in his place.*

"*Now these boys don't know discipline. The boy Raphael ... Miss Gerty grandson...look how hard that woman work to send him to school. Mother gone to England leave him a baby with her. Father must be spreading joy with bauxite money in Mandeville. Maybe Gert get something from the mother now and then but I hear she have a whole tribe in Brixton.*

"*Miss Gert scrub floor, clean filth in St Andrew so the boy could go to school. Boy get half scholarship to high school and form the fool. In my days only two boys from the district could get into high school and even then is backra mulatto children. The rest of us leave school in sixth standard or if the teacher see that you can take book he might decide to help you with your Jamaica Local Exams. My mother never had the money for me to go further than the first year of the Locals so I had to come to Kingston to see what I could find. Now that every and anybody getting into these big schools, standards lower. Boy have chance to make something of himself but still kicking football on the lane with dirty Trevor and them other riff raff. And after they take up the football, is the ganja and the locks and the gun. Well Miss Gert have funeral expense now.*"

The afternoon paper and the radio newscasts had the full police report on 18 year old Raphael Shand, alias Boy Blue, who was killed in a shoot out with a joint police military party and who was wanted by the police for questioning in connection with a spate of shootings in East Kingston.

When Marc left Chris at the New Kingston Hotel, he stayed inside for the afternoon. He checked in at the front desk then the bellhop helped him with his luggage as he rode the elevator to the ninth floor. The New Kingston was sandwiched between two taller towers. Chris Murphy's suite faced east giving him an unobstructed view of the Blue Mountain range which dominated the eastern end of Jamaica. Those must be the same blue, elegant mountains he saw driving in from the airport, he thought. The hills were scarred only in places where men in white drill shirts and shorts quarried marl. These were certainly different hills from the cockpitted terrain he flew over coming in from Montego Bay.

Marc had told him that the Blue Mountain coffee Chris loved grew in those mountains. "But you'll soon find out Chris my man, that coffee isn't the only Jamaican crop that's the world best," Marc had said. "You don't say," Chris said unimpressed. "People'll be coming up to you in the streets: 'Hey you want something to make you feel nice?' They're not kidding you."

"They grow coca here? They've got the white lady?"

"No to the first. To the second, yes. But that's not what I'm talking about. I'm talking Mary Jane."

"I've not messed with that shit since Nam. And I don't intend to get mixed up here."

"I remember when we first met you said you'd like to retire to your own business by the time you hit thirty...You must be thirty three now at least."

"That's what you're getting at? That's even worse, dammit."

"You've got diplomatic cover, Chris Murphy," Marc said, "and nobody's gonna mess with you. Besides, our government's the only sure link these guys have with the great decadent West right now."

The bedroom was air conditioned but when Chris stepped on the patio and felt the cool Caribbean breeze bathing his face, he stepped inside, turned off the unit and opened up the sliding glass doors. After a while he went down to the bar, got a few bottles of beer and came back to gaze at the cloud playing with the mountains in the distance and at the mansions in the foothills. He marvelled how from this position, the city he had just been driven through seemed to be more trees than buildings.

At 7 o'clock the phone rang. Murphy picked up the receiver.

"Mista Chris Murphy? This is the CID. We'd like you to come down to the lobby for five minutes or we're coming up fo' you."

"Go fry ice Fortesque," Chris responded to Marc's humour. "Be with you in a sec."

When he entered the lobby Marc jumped up alert and bowed solemnly, "M'sieur ambassadeur," mocking Murphy's stiff, jacket and tie look.

"Chris, you've been around these soirees long enough to know you don't need to be so stiff."

"O.K. I'll go up and change..."

"No, no. You can leave the jacket in the car. Around here jackets are on the way out. Asserting national culture...and it's hot here anyway."

They drove north up Knutsford Boulevard towards Trafalgar Road. As they did, Chris realised that the flanking high rise buildings displayed name plates like Citibank, Royal Bank of Canada, British American Insurance.

"Hey, I thought they had closed down all these multi nationals," he said as they drove past the IBM building.

"I told you, things aren't always as they seem."

"What are you saying, this is Hollywood and we're on a movie set?"

"You're partly right. Only, those aren't props and those guys are here to stay."

They filtered left at the traffic light and drove towards Hope Road. At the next light they waited in a row of three cars to turn right, up Hope Road.

"Not a bad town. At least the buildings are painted, unlike in Havana."

"Told you it's not bad."

When the light changed to green, the driver behind began blowing his horn.

"Cheese, the lights haven't switched a sec and some guy is honking down your tail."

Murphy enjoyed the rest of the drive up to Billy Dunn after they switched from the main thoroughfares. Only the occasional glaring headlight caused him to swear, "God, don't these dupes have dip switches?"

Billy Dunn was like most upper St Andrew hilltop residential areas. The houses were massive, usually two but sometimes three storeys with spacious rooms, luxurious furnishings, two cars in the garage (a third under the mango tree or possibly a motor bike), manicured lawns: little palaces. The only thing which marred the romance: burglar bars at every opening as suburbia lived in fear of the armed robber.

When the car swung into the gateway of the first secretary's residence, two policemen in trousers with blue side seams stepped back in a welcoming manner. They recognised the C.D. licence plate on Marc's car. He drove up the paved driveway and found a parking space between orderly parked cars, several with C.D. plates.

"Marc, you darling, come in." She saw Murphy coming behind him. "This must be the new guy on the block." She stuck out her hand, "Hi, I'm Beth Pearson."

"Delighted. Chris Murphy."

"Do feel welcome Chris." Looking at Marc, she said, "Don't allow him to spoil you."

"If he hasn't done it already, he won't be able to do it again," Chris grinned.

They walked through the wide room in which music tinkled faintly, voices buzzed and cigarette smoke swirled.

Beth was the first secretary's wife. The party was to welcome a new officer to the High

Commission. A waiter offered Marc and Chris drinks. They both took rum and Coca Cola. They milled. The High Commissioner was talking with the general manager of the local Bank of Nova Scotia.

"They've clearly gotta devalue," the manager was saying. "I don't know how long they can hold out but we certainly are not going to import goods from here at a dollar a pound when even with freight India gives us the same stuff for twenty, thirty cents. Soon they won't be able to compete even with other Caribbean islands."

"Well, what's going to happen is that the country will dry up. Bauxite alone can't keep them going and we certainly aren't going to subsidise nonsense. I've notified Ottawa..." The High Commissioner caught sight of the approaching soldier. "Ah...Captain Bogle, good to see you...We were just saying Jamaica should diversify its productive base, you know, concentrate all efforts on things you do best."

"I couldn't agree more," Bogle replied.

"It doesn't make sense to set up a massive processing plant here with all that expensive cooling equipment to make dried salted cod which sells for six dollars a pound, when we can sell you salted cod at 70 cents. On the other hand, no matter what we do, we won't be able to grow those lovely mangoes you have, so sell us those fresh, in syrups what have you...That's your priority."

"Speaking of cod," the bank manager interjected, "did you know that our bank had a branch in Kingston before we had one in

Toronto? We were here handling the salted fish business in the late 1800s..." He grinned at Bogle, "So you see our bank played a significant part in the development of your national dish, Captain."

"Ackee and saltfish as a national dish," Bogle said contemptuously. "I don't see how you can have a proven toxic substance, a poisonous fruit like ackee as a national dish. I don't eat it."

A waiter passed by with a tray of hors d'oeuvres. Ackee quiche, deviled eggs, stuffed chicken wings. "Lucky for us then," the High Commissioner said as he and the bank manager stacked saucers with ackee quiche and stuffed chicken wings.

Marc and Chris strolled over. After the introductions and exchanges, Bogle joined Marc and the engineer as they strolled into the enclosed quadrangular courtyard. There was a swimming pool in the centre. To one corner was a bar. They got drinks and were joined by the political attache from the American Embassy. He conformed very much to the stereotype in Black TV comedies: loud and overdressed.

"You guys planning a coup d'etat," he drawled. He entered and dominated the conversation. "The chief of immigration just asked me to help get visas for about a dozen of his relatives. How much do you think I should charge him? Ha ha ha! The general secretary of the ruling party just told me they might have to ask the Russians to help them with nuclear power technology if the CIA doesn't stop destabilising the economy and making it hard to buy fuel. He's flying a kite. I said 'Comrade, I'm just the spook by the door, I don't know what the hell's going on inside.' Hey! There's the general secretary of the opposition party. I'd better go and rap with her. Gotta send Washington a balanced report every month. And you never can tell, she may be in power again one day."

"Silly ass," Bogle said as the attache walked towards the woman. "But makes a damn good deal." Turning to Marc, "We've got to talk business Fortesque. Your friend in our line?"

"Put it this way, I haven't met the man who'd turn down twenty grand for an evening's work."

5 NEW WORLD TRIPPIN

When Christopher Columbus
lan pon de moon
an plant de American Union Jack
im neva find no Arawak.
Im sailing up to go down
an den find dat machine must touch groun
must come down.

Beep! Beep!
Radio wave
SPLASH!
Anada astronaut reach de grave
From anada one o Babylon plan.
A dread shout
Babel! Fable!
Man unable to find god in de sky
Can't tell I de same lie.

Neil arm strong, mighty man

Nimrod great
But who goin plant de sugar cane?
Martians goin feel de pain

123456
54321:
dis looney expedition
blast off wit Kremlin royal patent
Tranquil destination,
Skylab Santa Maria land
"A great step..."
But man nuh kind.

Dese Martians neva before seen
call dem green
an' rape angels to seed cane

So de dread call for St Marcus
to see de verdant face of god
pon a LSD trip
watch dollar an cent slip
an' madness gaining currency
While pickney belly empty
An not a soul raisin cain.

On July 23rd, it seemed as if the Rastafari had taken over Kingston. Red, gold and green knitted tams were everywhere. As one drove from the city centre downtown, up through Cross Roads to Half Way Tree, the tams were visible. The brethren and sistren were observing a holy day, the birthday of Emperor Haile Selassie I.

Not all the dreads or Rases belonged to any organisation and not all wore tams.

There were the Nyabinghi brethren who preferred to wear their dreads uncovered and to live in the rural hills, separate from Babylon, growing the food and vegetables they cooked and ate without salt: ital.

They held a ceremony, which was named after them, around a fire that was kept continually ablaze and around which there was drumming, chanting, smoking of ganja and ritual casting of stones or wood into the flames representing the destruction of Rome and Babylon.

There were Boboshanti or Bobo Dreads who praised a Trinity of Selassie, Marcus Garvey and their own leader Prince Emmanuel, who lived among them directing their daily industry: making brooms. These were humble dreads who mostly lived in a commune and who wore gowns over their traditional western style garb and carried their dreadlocks in a tight spiralling turban.

When the Boboshanti congregation met, brethren sat on one side of the assembly, sistren on the other, visitors at the back. No money or jewellery was allowed into the tabernacle, a 'temple guard' being responsible for their safety and eventual return after a service of hymn chants and praises of "Haile I, Selassie I, Emmanuel I, Jah RasTafari."

Then there were the Twelve Tribes of Israel which grouped black, white, brown, rich, poor, men, women into a single entity before dividing them according to birth month into the tribes of Jacob. Members paid dues and were arranged numerically for return to

Ethiopia, Zion, to land at Shashamane given by
the Emperor to the Ethiopian World Federation
for Western Blacks desirous of living on the
continent of Africa.

Yvonne belonged to the Rastafari Movemant
Theocracy, a more militant organisation than
the others in that they sought actively to get
representation in government a no no with
other Rastas who saw politics as politricks and
agitated for the entire community of the poor,
for welfare, health, schools.

What the organisations had in common was
the belief that Haile Selassie was Christ (God)
incarnate and that ganja was a holy sacrament
and a cure all which the governments of the
world should legalise. The peculiarity of
Rastafari talk showed up in the RMT's spelling
of MOVEMANT as opposed to MOVEMENT the
word 'man' signifying unity as against 'men' a
plural which signified division.

The RMT celebration was being held in the
hall of one of the many burial societies and
poor man's lodges which seemed to be all
located on Wildman Street a few blocks north
of Southside. It began with an exposition of art
and craft by the brethren and sistren, followed
later in the evening by devotions featuring
Nyabinghi type drumming, chanting and
reasoning, then in the night there was a fund
raising dance with music provided by a
powerful hi-fi sound system.

Yvonne had a stall in the celebration. She
displayed some of the woollen knitted tams and

vests as well as children's clothing which she made. She had been very good in needlework and textile classes at Homestead and the skills came in quite well when she and Jerry started out together. It supplemented well the earnings from his freelance writings.

A store in one of the shopping malls uptown gave her regular orders for infant clothing. She did not have a machine of her own at first but cut the garments and sewed them at a friend's house or if the order was sufficiently large, contracted some of the sewing to a small factory.

Mr and Mrs Stanley came to the celebration. Yvonne had invited them. Mr Stanley wore a floral dashiki and tan slacks looking refined and 'progressive' with his salt and pepper hair and spectacles. His wife wore a long floral evening dress and a head wrap.

They browsed around the stalls admiring the fare. She was more enthused and surprised than her husband at the high quality of the clay, leather and paintings and drawings.

She bought this and that marvelling, "The prices are so reasonable. Dear, could you rest these in the car for me?"

Yvonne watched them and felt a certain victory in their presence. Not that they had been any more Rastafarian than in the days before their rapprochement, and notwithstanding the dashiki and the long dress, her mother wore, her parents were not going back to Africa.

The fact was that the Stanleys were pragmatists as were everyone else: you either migrated or coped on the island. Coping meant going back to boiled green bananas and spinach instead of cornflakes or bacon and eggs for breakfast; discovering that ackee could go just as well with smoked red herring, salted mackerel or eaten by itself when there was no salted cod; remembering that mangoes were just as good as American apples and that cars could last for years and did not have to be changed annually. And being natural and at one with one's environment is what being Rastafari is about.

Mr Stanley was always the more tolerant of the parents in attitude towards Rastafari. Maybe because his father had been a Garveyite in the 1920s.

Mrs Stanley was a dark woman with wavy hair and proud of the Scottish or Irish ancestry which the hair represented. She was always on about what could or could not be done in her parents' house in St Ann.

"My mother was black but very cultured," she would tell Yvonne. "She used to accompany herself on the piano and sang so beautifully. And although she had ten of us my father would never allow her to work other than around the house. Well, he allowed her to give music lessons to children in the district, especially during the really rough times during the '20s. He was Scottish you know, but he was born here."

From an uncle, Yvonne learned that her grandfather had about fifty acres of land in St Ann. The old man used to be a planter and dealer in animals: cattle, horses, mules. He was one of two illegitimate children born to a Rev Kerr who came out to Jamaica in the last century. The reverend gentleman had other children by his wife but these two bastards, whose existence Mrs Kerr knew nothing about, were named Clarke after their black mother.

Of Mrs Stanley's generation, one brother had gone to Cuba in the old days and they never heard from him again. Another had gone to Panama, married and had a big family. He came to Jamaica once or twice and his daughter visited a few times as well. Yvonne's mother, now in her fifties was the last child of her parents.

In the Stanleys' home in Vineyard Town, three big photographs hung on the walls. There were two bust portraits: of Mrs Stanley's mother, black with wide, sleepy eyes; father, mulatto with straight white hair, twisted moustache and pale eyes. The third picture was of Mr Stanley's father, black, balding, round faced, monocled, black jacket, pin stripe vest, white shirt, (gold?) watch chain and perched on a tall stool or chair. All three pictures were faded and the subjects reminded you of those you saw on the obituaries page of the newspapers.

At the RMT celebration things were warming up. A group of drummers, about five sat in a semi circle on low stools. They played the Rastafari heartbeat pattern of drumming and raised some traditional chants. Some were taken from the 'Redemption Songs' hymnal mistakenly called 'Sankey' by most fundamental church believers. Others were contemporary reggae tunes like 'By the Rivers of Babylon'.

The drumming went on for about half an hour then the executive members and the 'elder dreads' took their seats on the stage. The 12 or so men and two women sat on metal folding chairs to the left of the drummers. It was an open air hall like a cinema: walled entrance with small front office leading onto an open rectangular court with rows of chairs occupied by the congregation and guests; the far white wall behind the stage decorated with a red, gold and green rainbow hung with portraits of Haile Selassie, Marcus Garvey and past and present African leaders.

None of the brethren seated on the stage was smoking but the smell of ganja pervaded the air as smoke rose above groups of men standing by the stalls on the perimeter of the hall.

"Greetings!" a lanky dread on the stage shouted into a microphone. "Greetings!" the crowd chorused. "Greetings in the name of our God and King Emperor Haile Selassie the First whose birthday I an' I is gathered to celebrate."

"Selassie I!" the believing crowd responded emotionally.

"Yes I," the dread began, "Babylon tell I an' I that December 25th is Christmas but them same one turn it roun' an' call it X mas so it plain that them wrong from the start and them know that them wrong.

"Even though this is a festive occasion brothers and sisters, these are perilous times for I an' I. These is not the days of Dungle and Back O Wall from whence I an' I rise up in this dispensation; no. For I sight even I an' I brethren driving 'roun town in Benz and BMW but I an' I still not to take that to mean the struggle over.

"Some people even saying how Rasta rich and can afford to travel back to Africa. But even though the situation in Jam down is almost like South Africa, I an' I not dealing with emigration, I an' I calling on Babylon to repatriate I an' I so that I an' I who never requested to be in the West can be redeemed of the stigma of slavery. Physical slavery done but economic and mental slavery still have us in shackles."

As Mrs Stanley listened she thought why these intelligent, middle class young people were attracted to this silly religion, calling a man God. "Maybe it's just a rebellious phase like the hippies in America," she thought.

Yvonne was thinking how much she missed Jerry. This was the first celebration he was missing. Most certainly he would be sitting with the executive. His name was bound to be mentioned several times during the evening as the martyr of the organisation.

...Jerry had gone back to the university to complete his degree, citing the emperor's emphasis on education. He loved the challenge, the feel of being the dreadlocks in the class, alone against Rome. In sociology classes he particularly loved the thrust and parry with the lecturer... "Maybe this is as good a time as any for Caribbean leaders to begin looking whether the media, particularly the electronic media, should not reflect more of what is happening within our societies than bombarding us with the garbage of the Western world."

"No Sah, I can't agree with that totally. If anything we need to get more information than we get now. I know that people in New York and them places more aware of what going on in Africa and even here in the Caribbean than we ourself know. If anything I would say get more of the better quality information and programmes from outside but not less."

"But Jerry, wouldn't you agree that the decadence, the crime, the drugs are a result of our peoples aping what they see on television, on the movie screens?"

"No Sah. Crime in Jamaica is caused by economic hardship and political victimisation. You have to come into the ghetto and see it. Ah don't say you don't have guys that just going after the big bucks but most crime is native. The use of guns? Politricks!

"Ah don't know if you include ganja as drugs but the herb has always been a part of this culture. Come with the Africans and East Indians. Ah tell you something, coke and cigarette smoking, them Westerners come right down here and get the habits from the native Amerindians, and without TV." The class laughed.

"So how do you explain the drift from traditional values and norms...the move away from communal living towards urbanisation?"

"There was urbanisation before the 'West' came into being you know Sah. And you see all the argument about communal living...let's face facts: no Caribbean government has ever actively promoted Africanism. The reason for the Caribbean's existence is to be Europe's plantations overseas. Independence hasn't changed the minds of the people from what they see as success: schooling, a nice office job, marriage, house and a car."

"What do you think of Burnham's efforts in Guyana in being cautious about introducing television and promoting African and Amerindian institutions alongside those of the East Indians'?"

"First of all you see Sah, I an' I de Rastafari don't support witchcraft, voodoo and obeah whether from Europe or Africa but I would prefer not to say anything about Guyana since all I have to go on is newspaper reports. The difference between being Rastafari and being Jamaican is that I an' I is strivin for a universal, no, a I niversal culture of using the best of all for the good of all."

Jerry didn't naturally speak Rastafarian. It was received and took as much conscious effort as it did the average Jamaican to speak Standard English. He grew up speaking standard middle class Jamaican English.

Grandpa Henry never spoke Jamaican dialect; just the plain, unaccented standard, and that was one reason Jerry never had problems with English in school like many of his compeers.

Jerry was born out of wedlock. His father had gone off to study law in England and Jerry's mother, an Afro East Indian who had worked with the Henrys, deposited him with his grandfather and disappeared to make sure the boy got a good schooling and did not experience the poverty she knew.

Dr Henry was an upstanding man in the community. A devout church man, he never missed a Sunday service. As a grandmaster in a masonic lodge, his friends were bankers, lawyers, and successful men with no visible means of support.

He treated his grandson, who he thought resembled him but for his colour, with more compassion than did his wife, who Jerry thought hated him for his dark complexion.

Instinctively he knew that he must excel academically if he were to succeed in life and so he absorbed the books in his grandfather's library. At 10, he won a free place to Jamaica College in the scholarship examinations for 11 year olds to enter high school.

At 15, Jerry passed eight ordinary level subjects in his Cambridge General Certificate of Eduation and then some unusual events occurred.

First his mother suddenly appeared at Grandpa Henry's one Sunday morning. She had been only a hazy memory but now there she was in her bandana head wrap, silver and black hair exposed at the right of her forehead, come to claim her son.

"Marning doctor, Ah come fo' Jerry sar," she said when Dr Henry responded to the rap on the door of the back porch.

"Mabel, is that you? Good to see you after all these years. Come in."

"Is all right sar, Ah will just stay out here while the boy pack sar."

"But you can't just come and grab him like that. He's still in school you know."

"Yes sar, but 'im is 16 now sar. Him big enough an' can work now sar. Ah don't want 'im to burden yu no more an' Ah could do with de help miself now sar. Can't get no work an' Ah have five more children an' none of dem father is aroun'..."

Jerry walked up behind his grandfather, "Dada, who is that?"

"Oh, Jerry, come and meet your mother..."

Jerry saw glazed eyes staring at him and heard a distant shrill, "Pack bwoy. Yu have to come and help yu old mother."

"Dada send her away!" he screamed as he rushed to his room and locked the door.

"Look, Mabel, I think you had better come back another day while Jerry is at school and let's sit down and discuss the whole matter."

For the next term Jerry's school grades fell as he pondered daily whether the little mad witch in the bandana would turn up and embarrass him in the company of his friends in the lower sixth form. For three months, he went straight home when classes broke at 2:15 p.m. and never hung out with the guys at the record shop in Cross Roads.

Then another thing happened. His father

wrote to say he was coming home to set up his legal practice. Jerry was relieved that may be if he went to live with his father, the mad woman would at least not have any more right to claim him.

But when the lawyer, his English wife and half caste children arrived from London and she said "At least Jerry'll be able to help me around the house," Jerry heard even more contempt in her tone than in his grandmother's sarcasm. He was happy to stay with his grandfather and for a long time he saw or heard nothing of his mother again.

But Jerry was upset by the discovery that his Christian grandfather was performing abortions which was the reason for the popularity of his surgery among women.

About a year and a half after his father came home, Jerry was waiting at the bus stand in Half Way Tree for the bus. In white paint was scrawled on the low red brick park wall across the street, "Birth control is a plan to kill black people."

Two women were engrossed in a conversation next to him, oblivious of his presence.

"Ah pregnant so Ah have to go an' see Doctor Henry to set things right," he overheard.

The one remaining pure spirit in his life was tarnished.

"There is no pure soul," he wrote in the first of what was to be many poems. Some questioned his own blackness. In this more contemplative mood, it was the momentum of his early brilliance that took Jerry through his advanced level exams and into the university.

When Jerry graduated he applied for a government job advertised in the newspapers. During the job interview the bearded government functionary told him the job was political. "Not party political," he said "but insofar as it is to promote the programmes of the government of the day it is partisan."

The man wanted to know Jerry's position on anti imperialism, communism and the Soviet Union. They argued over whether there was such a phenomenon as cultural imperialism, Jerry saying yea, the man, nay, that there was one imperialism and that it was economic; that what Jerry spoke of was cultural hegemony. He did not even look at Jerry's diplomas and newspaper clippings which he had brought along.

"Thanks for coming to the interview comrade," the man said. "I an' I come black," Jerry thought mockingly as he stood and left the room.

Jerry had decided that they should not remove from Southside immediately, although things were looking up for the family economically since he graduated. He continued his freelance writing and did some part time teaching at a high school. Also he started organising an adult education class in an old Chinese shop building on the block. It had been abandoned by the owners as had the premises where Jerry and Yvonne lived.

The youth of the area called him Prof. He would urge them to set aside politics and unite as Africans. It seemed he was getting through to a few with his campaign of unity in the community as they would now come and sit and reason with him on evenings instead of idling under the street lamps.

About 11 o'clock one night it happened. Jerry and Yvonne were making love in their back room and Tafari was asleep in the front. A yard with forty odd people never really sleeps so the footsteps outside did not disturb the lovers' rhythm. Suddenly there was a banging on the door. "Open up! Security!" There was a banging again.

"Take it easy officer," Jerry shouted putting on his underwear and hauling on his trousers. Yvonne was annoyed. They were used to the raids but it had never disturbed their love making before. A bang on the door again.

"What wrong with them?" Yvonne asked.

Jerry got to the door and opened it. Tafari awakened and thought he was dreaming. "Yes officer, can I help you sah?" said Jerry.

Two men in battle green fatigues were there, one in police uniform and a fourth neatly dressed in plain clothes. They were all armed.

"Gervaise Henry?" the man in plain clothes asked.

"Yes" Jerry answered.

"Gervaise Anthony Henry?"

"Yes," he replied again. Yvonne had dressed and come up behind him.

"Yu hear 'bout the killing in Bournmouth?"

"The accountant gunman shoot last week?"

"Same one. We come to talk to yu 'bout it."

"I can only tell you what I hear on the radio

and read in the newspaper."

Some of the others who lived in the yard peeked through windows. A few who were in the yard using the stand pipe or the bathroom gathered to see what was happening. One said, "Unno leave de dread, 'im nuh mix up inna nutten."

"All o' unno get inside!" the man in police uniform ordered the spectators. They sauntered off in various directions.

"Yes Jerry," the man rejoined, "we want a search."

"You have a warrant or any form of I.D?"

"We nuh need dat yu nuh." And they started into the room except one of those in fatigues.

"Jerry, yu apply to government recently fo' a job?"

"Yes."

"So where yu work now?"

"Ah teach part time and do some free lance writing."

"An' full time gunman?" the man in plain clothes said wryly.

"You mixing me up with somebody else."

The man in police uniform was prowling around the shanty and from the back room came a shout, "Wait, wha' dis Jerry, collie? Yu a herb dealer?"

The interrogator said, "We come fo' yu fo' one thing but we get yu fo' something else Jerry. Come wit' we to de car."

"Firstly, Ah don't sell ganja but everyone know that Rastaman smoke," he said "And secondly, the man dem say dem is police but Ah don't see any I.D."

"Yes," Yvonne chimed in, "where is yu I.D.?

"Shut up 'ooman!" one said.

Tafari started crying.

"I.D in de car," the interrogator said.

"O.K, I will come and see it," Jerry suggested.

"Alright."

"No Jerry," Yvonne cried. "Make them go and come back with it."

"Is alright," Jerry said stepping through the midst of them towards the door.

"Don't run Jerry!" the interrogator shouted as Jerry set one foot out the door.

Alarmed he looked back to see an automatic hand gun spitting fire at him. Life raced before Jerry as he stumbled and fell. Yvonne was screaming. Tafari was crying, "Them shoot Daddy Jerry. Them shoot Daddy Jerry."

The men picked up the body and walked to the gate, Yvonne screaming behind them. A crowd gathered in the street at the sound of the gunshots. The men dumped the body in an unmarked jeep and fired shots in the air as the buzzing crowd pressed forward. The crowd scattered. The men entered the jeep and drove off. "The only good communis' is a dead communis'," one of the men joked in the jeep.

Yvonne rushed to the public hospital to see if they had taken Jerry there. They had not. She went to Central Police Headquarters, a few blocks from their home. They did not know of any operation in that area and took a statement from Yvonne. The next morning Jerry's body was found on South Camp Road.

The political parties condemned the brutal

terrorist killing. A coroner's inquest ruled that he was murdered by persons unknown.

That was early in the year and as the violence escalated the government declared a state of emergency because of the "terrorism planned by the opposition in collusion with outside forces".

Mr and Mrs Stanley left the celebration at about nine o'clock that night. They had heard speaker after speaker hit out against the world and injustice and had been getting dizzy from a contact high. Yvonne and Tafari walked with them to their car.

"Why don't you let Tafari come up with us tonight; he's not going to school tomorrow," Mrs Stanley said.

"Yeah!" Tafari pranced. "Can I mamma?" He was thinking of the TV he'd be able to watch at his grandparents since he had none at home.

"Yes Tafari, you can go with your grandma and grandpa."

"By the way," Mrs Stanley said to her daughter. "Why don't you move out of that godforsaken place. The cottage at home is empty now and I don't want any of those modern day tenants who don't pay rent and curse you on top of it."

"That's the reason you want us to come there Ma?"

"Heavens, no child. You know I don't want any grandchild of mine growing up in that hell thinking THAT is his heritage."

"We'll talk about it Ma," Yvonne said as her mother got into the car.

"Night Vonnie," her father said, "We really would like you at home."

"Tomorrow, mama," Tafari said.

The murder of Jerry had a deep effect on Yvonne. She swore to avenge his death. Jerry had been her personal messiah, saving her from a life dictated by urban middle class parents whose rule was that children must be seen and not heard and daughters must be reined until their wedding day. This regime had put solitude and stubbornness in her from early and would be displayed in the frequent quarrels with her father: over whether she could go to a matinee movie with girls from her form during the mid term break, or a friend's birthday party.

There would be an argument then Yvonne would shut up an silently ignore her father's tirade in which he explained why his action was for her own good. Then the silence would sting him because he interpreted, correctly, that it was obstinacy. He wanted words to know her thoughts to gauge her actions.

Jerry freed her even though Rastafari was a male centred movement and she had become more his female half than herself. But the new activities were, to her, her own, because she followed of her own free will. And with Jerry, she spoke her deep seated fears and digested the honey of his consoling philosophy.

She spoke to the sisters in the organisation but not many were her friends because even in this egalitarian society, the code of knowing ones place survived and many respected her regal posture and Jerry and her own middle class background. Only Carol, one of the two friends with whom she had attended the grounation at the university and who had also walked the way of Rastafari, was close and knew some of Yvonne's thoughts. Only Carol and her "king man" Trevor visited Yvonne frequently at the yard and only Carol saw Yvonne cry over the loss of Jerry and heard her swear that he would be avenged.

When Jerry was alive many more brethren and their "queens" visited and the people in the yard greeted them all, "Hail dread," or "Hail lion." The roughnecks in the lane did not molest them because they were identified by their red, gold and green tams and big buttons with a portrait of Haile Selassie. Once, a young hot head attempted to attack a brethren on his way to visit Jerry but a higher ranks shouted: "Leave de dread alone, yu no see a one humble lion. Ah de Prof brethren."

And there was the "tracing" matches in the yard which Yvonne escaped until now. Ivorene, who many said was a lesbian, and cussed any woman who she could not get, found some way to verbally lambaste all the other females. She would start a quarrel waiting at the stand pipe awaiting her turn with "Yu wet me yu nuh. Yu nuh believe me a somebody to?" She would proceed to tell the person things about their mother and other family they never dreamt of and a thousand and one other low down reasons the person was the way they were.

One evening she attacked Yvonne over the length of time she took in the bathroom: "But a wha' you could a have fe wash off so, 'cause yu nuh have no man a sleep wid yu a night again." It hurt Yvonne to the core and when she stepped from the bathroom with her towel and bundle of soiled clothes, she retorted: "Sorry to hold you up Ivorine but if man is the reason to bathe you would have no need to bathe at all." Yvonne said nothing else but Ivorine cussed for the next hour. "...All your likkle bway, yu go on like fe 'im shit nuh stink, 'cause you wouldn't even mek 'im play wid de other likkle pickney dem inna de yard..."

Yvonne closed her door, sat on her bed and cried as Tafari did his home work. Jerry where are you? the terror in the street. The terror in this house this yard. The poverty to which I was not born. The victory of daddy who doesn't even gloat "I told you so" so that I could find a reason... Then Tafari said, "Mama, don't cry. When I grow big I going get a house like grandpa own and you can live there."

After Tafari was born, his grandparents amended their attitude towards Yvonne. Not immediately after he was born, because they never saw him until he was about a year old. They bumped into Yvonne downtown as she sought material to sew clothes for Tafari.

"Oh, isn't he cute," Mrs Stanley chirped as she timidly stroked his hair. Mr Stanley stood stone faced. It was he who had insisted that Yvonne would have to leave home because of her pregnancy. "...He looks just like you."

Inside Mr Stanley was burning up. He adored the child as much as his wife did but it was a tough compromise to show it.

"How are you managing my dear? You have to come home...She is our daughter, this is our grandchild. We can't allow them to be battering about Kingston like destitutes Ken." She began to cry when the baby reached out his hand and touched her cheek and her spectacles.

"Thanks but no thanks mama," Yvonne said. "When I really needed your support, where was it? The only person I saw was Jerry and at least his grandfather didn't put him out."

"Yvonne you don't understand. Your father and I, we tried to give you everything. When your brother and sister were growing up, we didn't have it to give them. That's why Trevor had to work to pay his way through college as did Joy. They never returned from the States. You were all we had," Mrs Stanley was sobbing.

"Mama, is Rastafari I dealing with now yu nuh, and I sure you not going deal with that so is best we just let life be."

It was then that Mrs Stanley noticed her daughter's dreadlocks for the first time; a single short lock protruding at the right side from beneath the colourful head wrap Yvonne wore.

"Oh Yvonne you haven't...What have you done with your hair? Oh my God. Ken where did we go wrong?" Mrs Stanley turned to her husband.

"Please come home Yvonne. What did we do to you? Don't cause us any more pain..."

"You heard what she said, 'let life be'," said Mr Stanley in a manner partly consoling, partly hurt and somewhat contemptuously.

"Where are you living child?" she asked.

"I'm not a child mama. You've helped make me a woman. Why do you want my address; will you visit us in the ghetto?"

But there was a rapprochement. Yvonne told them where she lived and agreed to visit them in Vineyard Town on a Sunday.

The whole family visited: Yvonne in her flowing African gown, Jerry in a dashiki and jeans and Tafari in a red gold and green woollen tam and a blue outfit Yvonne had made.

The ice was really broken during that visit with the women busy in the kitchen and the men in the living room discussing Africa and Rastafari, the baby perched on his grandfather's lap.

"Haile Selassie is a great man and descended from the line of David and all that but I can't see him as God," said Mr Stanley.

"You have to come to that realisation of Jah being all in all. No one can teach you that," said Jerry. "We are saying that this is Christ in his kingly character...The conquering lion, no more lamb to the slaughter."

"But why the hair? You don't have to knot up your hair like that. Haile Selassie doesn't have locks. When he came here in 1966, he cried when he saw the terrible looking locksmen and he himself said he was not God."

"He never said he wasn't God. He said, 'Read the Book of Light and you will see.' I and I wear the dreadlocks because we vow the vow of the Nazarine. As a youth Selassie I wore the dreadlocks."

"You claim that Marcus Garvey prophesy about Selassie but do you know that Garvey cursed him as a coward because he went to England and left his people when Italy invaded Ethiopia in 1936?"

Jerry fumbled and said the exile was a strategic move and mentioned prophecy about England being Ephraim, the Israelite half tribe descended from Joseph, and therefore being an ally of Ethiopia. And he said Garvey was only John the Baptist and only condemned the king in a moment of emotional anger.

"My father was a Garveyite you know, and the back to Africa that Garvey preached was a different thing to what you fellows are talking about. He was talking about building up an economic empire; not going back there in a mass to try and find what tribe you come from, for none of us can trace that. We are all mixed up down here."

"I agree that Garvey wasn't just dealing with physical repatriation, but we have to deal with that too as part of the redemption of Africa because our foreparents never came here willingly so we have a right to return just like the Israelis going back to Palestine."

During a talk on another Sunday, Mr Stanley told Jerry, "You know what our problem is? It's that black people don't want to be involved in business. As soon as we get educated we think that business, selling is degrading."

He told Jerry that some of those who believed in business were not bold enough to develop and grow.

"I know a man in St Catherine with a little tyre repair shop about 15 years now. His children used to help him and these days when I'm driving through the countryside, I don't even see him again. One of his boys take over but not even a coat of paint on the little shack since I passing there 15 years.

"But look at the Syrians and the Lebanese. I knew when Hanna was pushing cloth on a bicycle around Kingston in the '30s. Now the family has how many big businesses across the island and all of them involved in some way or other.

"When I left the army in '49, I took my pension in a lump sum and start a little hardware business. Now my children, two of them gone to university in America and they not interested in my business. When I gone who is going to take over? Vonnie? She going to Africa."

As Tafari grew, Mr Stanley hoped his grandson would one day inherit his business. He would say to his wife, "The boy is so bright. I'm really glad they didn't decide to locks his hair. You know their organisation and the other one, 12 Tribes, is sending people to Africa?! I really hope they don't haul him off there too."

Tafari himself was harbouring a fear about the Africa trip because he had reasoned that since the members were sent by numbers and his number was 301 and his parents 120 and 121, he would certainly be left alone in Jamaica. At one stage he even told his friends that he would soon be leaving school to start working, since he thought he would have to fend for himself. That was one reason he clung so closely to his grandparents.

At about midnight when the dance session of the celebration was in full swing, the soldiers and police came. The sound system disc jockey was in command pouring out lyrics over a 'dub' version of the Abyssinians hit 'Satta a massagana'. Some couples were dancing rub a dub style, resembling making love standing and fully dressed. But most of the crowd danced by themselves. The men stood 'skanking' by themselves and the women, most in long skirts, did the same.

At a dance like this only reggae music was played. Sometimes the sound system operator would play a dozen or more versions of one song. It was in the tradition of the 'sounds men'.

In the 50s and up to 1962, when dances used to begin and end with 'God Save the Queen', the sounds men used to compete to get first presses of new American records. And when local recording began, the contest intensified with some sounds men building their own powerful amplifiers and going into the studios to cut single copies of a tune. Then they'd probably get a trombonist like Don Drummond to blow a solo on the rhythm tracks which would set the dance hall ablaze.

The resident DJ called a toaster then would use that dub to drive the nail into the coffin of other competing sound systems.

By the time the Rasta percussion and beat had been infused with the traditional mento and the horns and bass progressions of jazz to create first ska, then rocksteady, then reggae, the dance hall had been the haven of the poor.

When the lyrics of a ghetto poet like Bunny Wailer backed by a heavy pounding bass line plucked a responsive chord in a ghetto youth saturated with beer and herb, he would shout, "JAH!" If he had a gun in his waist, he would pull it and fire in the air to "shout Jah louder".

This did not usually happen at a Rasta dance, as the visiting gunmen generally behaved themselves there; but to the security forces a dance is a dance is a dance, so they made surprise entrances to them.

"Security awn ya, so jus' cool inna yu corner," the DJ crooned, alerting patrons as a record faded. Before the next record started he said, "Please cooperate wit' de forces crowd o' people."

Clavel Smith in his battle green fatigues and helmet with his M16 rifle was among the soldiers. As he walked through the crowd towards the hi fi set, he saw Yvonne dancing alone along with a group of women in a lit area.

He was glad. Now he knew where he was likely to find her away from her home. The Rastafari Movemant Theocracy held dances all over the city to raise funds.

The soldiers left shortly after they arrived and the dance ended at daybreak without any drama.

6 AFRICA SITS...

...below a cut stone steeple and the cross
in a small corner of the ville
(green and cool and elevated
this town in mountain country
main street a pine cooled avenue
close cropped lawn and everything in place
elates the parvenu)
stooping
in a corner clustered
green and yellow
bananas, oranges
unaromatic wafts of beef and bird
by the pound, heavy.
women, some bandana'd
charcoal or chocolate;
colours and bodies and shouts and scents
"Fifty cent fi skellion
fifty cent..."
where wealth and poverty

meat and hunger congregate
beneath a stone brick cross she sits.

"*Rock of ages,*" a voice called and a chorus of voices echoed the line. "*Cleft for me.*"

The discordant singers drawled the response: a dirge. They were gathered at Miss Gerty's house to drink white rum and eat fried sprat and hard dough bread. It was the ninth night since the death of Boy Blue and her relatives, friends and even those with whom she frequently had big cuss outs in her yard had gathered to console her at this 'nine night' ceremony.

Every night since the shooting there had been 'set ups' with constant eating and drinking. It was like a carnival in the lane. Somebody had wired up a sound system with big speaker boxes thumping some heavy reggae rhythms. 'Rankings' from all over the fringing slums who supported the same party turned up. Some came on big four cylinder Japanese motorbikes, others in fancy cars.

The woman who owned the shop in which Mr Hudson sat stocked up on cartons of beer after the first night and did a roaring business. Rankings always ordered beer by the crate so that their minions could have a good time and be impressed by their high status.

One ranking brought a white woman on his bike. Her face looked young but her eyes were drooped and arms shrivelled. They were a well known couple in the underworld community and it was rumoured that her arms were that way from shooting needles up them. The man seldom spoke and they said his super cool was from snorting cocaine.

On the third night of the revelry, the night Boy Blue's spirit was supposed to have risen, his grandmother sent and asked that the music be toned down a bit. "At least since unno say unno is 'im fren, unno could at least show 'im some respec'," Miss Gerty said.

In the shop spirits were high. "Wha' 'appen old man, yu want a beer?" one ranking asked Mr Hudson who sat in his usual corner.

"No thank you sah," he replied curtly.

The ranking grinned not understanding Hudson's attitude and shouted over the counter to the attendant, "Set up de old man wit' a soft drink sweetie."

"You don't hear a say no thank you!" Mr Hudson yapped.

Under his breath he grumbled, "*All of you is damn thieves and murderers, 'bout unno is contractor. Contractor to kill... Look at this lovely country. Is the damn politicians and these riff raff mashing it up. From they start this nonsense about rationing public works according to party support is nothing but worries.*

"*Look what happen back when they were building Sandy Gully. You know how many men lose their life, not from any of the bulldozers, but through politics.*

"*And it get worse since they say we independent. We free to do foolishness. Everything change up. Foreshore Road is Marcus Garvey Drive, Back o' wall is Tivoli Gardens and you have to join a party to live there. None of those people who them bulldoze off the dump get any house. They change from pound shillings and pence to dollars and cents and the price of everything skyrocket.*

"Now the boy Raphael...No more than 17 or 18, 'bout he is contractor. Boy didn't finish school. But I told Miss Gerty that she should send the boy to England to his mother the moment I see him start getting mixed up with bad company..."

The singing had stopped in Miss Gerty's house. Somebody switched on her stereogram and put a Pat Boone record on the turntable. It made a frying sound before the song began *"I come to the garden alone.."* with the frying underneath.

Raphael had not yet been buried. Miss Gerty had sent a telegram to her daughter in England: POLICE KILL RAPHAEL STOP I NEED YOUR HELP STOP. She was hoping that the boy's mother would be coming and would bring a burial suit and generally help with the cost of the funeral. But only that morning she got the equally skimpy reply: SORRY TO HEAR STOP HOPE TO SEND SOMETHING SOON STOP.

Miss Gerty knew what that meant. Her daughter had met a Guyanese in England and never told him about Raphael in Jamaica. Even after the nuptials the man still thought Raphael was her nephew for whom she sometimes sent something. She therefore could not justify to her husband sending one hundred pounds for the funeral of a dead nephew, or even consider leaving England to visit that war zone for the funeral of a mere relative.

Grandma Gert was grieved. Her eyes were red although she was not crying. A woman from the lane crossed the room to where Miss Gert sat on the bed. The room was fetid with rum and fried fish and sweat.

"Miss Gert, mi glad to see how de people dem support yu in yu hour of grief. Is so we must band together all de time."

"Yes mi dear. Mi Have to t'ank unno." She thought, "Who is going to pay for all this rum and fish and light bill."

"It really sad what happen to Boy Blue."

"Raphael ears too hard. Me did till him dat him need a read up an' a bush bath. Me say, 'Raphael, even de big man dem doin' it for yu can't reach nuhwhere in dis country before some red eye somebody gone to obeahman to pull yu down.' But him say, 'Granny, I don't believe in dem duppy and obeah argument.' Well, see where him is now sake o' hard ears."

"So you hear from yu daughter?"

At the mention of the word daughter, Miss Gert let out a wail. She was thinking of the telegram which had promised nothing specific. She had had to make withdrawals from her burial society deposits and from her rainy day savings account. Her grandson's body couldn't stay at the morgue any longer and he didn't deserve a pauper's grave in a cheap wooden box. A casket costing a few hundred dollars was one burden. The other was the constant stream of people willing to offer trust (credit) since the death.

They had a funeral service at the cemetery chapel for Raphael 'Boy Blue' Shand after they drove the body in a hearse down the lane for the final time. The entire lane except Mr Hudson and Yvonne attended the funeral conducted by the 'Bishop' of the Church of God and Saints of Christ Zion Apostolic faith.

The bishop, ornately dressed in black gown with red waistband and blue head wrap, preached a scorching sermon.

"...Lord you see what greed and envy do to this little country! Red eye! Want it want it. Anything yu neighbour have you must have it too. But yu see the rich man in him castle, yu don't know how much headache, how much bad heart, how much sleepless nights him is having.

"How everybody going to have? The bible say the poor will always be with us. Yu don't know how some get. Some t'ief. Yu going t'ief? Or yu going beg? The Good Book say don't t'ief. The Good Book say don't borrow.

"Is want it want it why all this problem 'bout here. Is want it want it why this young man in this wooden box here before us today.

"Somebody want all the votes. Somebody want all the power so them can take what people work years for and make somebody else rich in a day.

"Them say them going give we more freedom but my Lord say all freedom is in him. He alone can deliver and he will deliver us.

"Too much man want to follow and too much man want to lead. But Lord you are my deliverer. You make me poor but you make me free. Our foreparents were slaves but we are free.

"Lord deliver these people from Satan. Deliver them O Lord from the hands of the oppressor who want to bring back slavery."

Rapturous singing, hand clapping, tambourine shaking and electric guitar strumming began as he ended:

"We shall have a grand time, up in heaven...

Walking with the angels, talking with the angels

We shall have a grand time up in heaven, have a grand time..."

The top rankings fired their guns in the air in salute to Boy Blue after the bishop said his final "ashes to ashes, dust to dust".

The funeral was on a week day; the same day Yvonne moved back to Vineyard Town; a quiet late afternoon when many of the partisans were not around to target her as a deserter. Because hers and Boy Blue's vote would be two less for that side in an election.

****

The baby Chev drove through the winding country roads overhung by tall trees. Lazy cattle grazed in the shade in pastures with barbed wire fences. The pastures were an undulating carpet of green. Marc Fortesque and the High Commission's public affairs officer were going to St Ann to the hamlet of

Aboukir where the Canadians were helping a youth group to set up self help cottage industries.

When they stopped in the village square and the rushing wind caused by movement stopped, the air was dry and hot. Not many people moved about. It had the feeling of Tombstone or some such town from a western. The youth club house resembled a small church building.

The young men and women were on time for their meeting. Marc had brought good news. The money for the project had been approved and things could get rolling. After the meeting Marc and the public affairs officer were treated to refreshment before they began the 50 mile journey back to Kingston.

"Rosie you don't mind my stopping briefly before we get back to Kingston, do you?" he asked.

She wanted to get back to Kingston before dark but she said "Certainly not Marc."

As they approached Brown's Town, the hub of that district of St Ann, he took the car off the main road and drove about half a mile then turned into a wide gate that led to a rambling old country house on a knoll. The greenery of the place and the house with its shingled roof and veranda which completely encircled the building were seductive; made you want to stay there on a hot, dry day.

"Marc, yu find yu way," Captain Bogle grinned as he descended the steps at the front of the house and headed, rum glass in hand, towards the car. He leaned by the window and saw the young lady. "Hi," he said.

"Do you know Rosie Clarke? Miss Clarke is our public affairs lady," Marc said. "Rosie, Ruddy Bogle captain in your army. But you don't have to salute him Rosie," he joked. Rosie and Bogle exchanged pleasantries and he invited them to get out of the sun.

They got out of the car and climbed the steps. Captain Bogle, dapper in his casual wear, lagged behind.

"Ivan!" he shouted to a man brushing a hedge around the foundations, "where is Randy? Get him to pick some jelly coconuts for Mr Fortesque and the lady." Bounding up the steps, he said, "Marc, yu ever had rum and coconut water? Yu going have some today, because you not a whisky man like me. You love your rum."

"You're in command," Marc said.

They all sat on the veranda in Adirondack chairs. A cool breeze blew and brought the aromatic whiff of pimento.

"I like your house, Captain," Rosie said.

"Yu like it? Thank yu. This property has been in the family for maybe two hundred years but I just bought it off a relative who decided that he couldn't take Jamaica anymore. Gone to Florida. But I want to see which politician going get me off of here.

"With all due respect dear," he said to Rosie she was black "my family has been in this country fo' hundreds of years and I not going to allow no 'fly by night' politician to hand over so many generations of hard work to any 'struggling masses'.

"I know that you not one o' them communist yu hear mi dear," he said restraining his emotion, "but..."

"Hey captain, where's your man with my coconut water?" Marc broke in to diffuse the tension.

"Oh gosh, you must excuse my bad manners my dear," Bogle said to Rosie, "I never offered you a drink. What are you having?"

"Something soft thanks. I always seem to love lemonade when I'm out in the country."

"We have wet sugar yu know..."

"Oooh, I love wet sugar lemonade."

"I'll just have them mix some for you," he said excusing himself. Shortly after he returned, a black middle aged woman came out with a tray holding the brown lemonade, red rum, a pitcher of coconut water and a bowl of ice. After the drinks they had a late lunch inside the big antique furnished dining room where the wooden floor glistened.

This was not the original house built by George Bogle, a mulatto who started buying pieces of land in the area in the 1820s. George's father had come out to the West Indies in the late 18th Century to seek his fortune as an estate attorney. Things didn't go too well for him in Barbados where there were not many absentee landlords, so he decided to press up to Jamaica where an in law put him in charge of a 1,000 acre estate most of which was in sugar cane and a sugar factory.

The estate also included 120 slaves, almost all of whom were born there. The owner who inherited the land and people, lived in a fashionable London district, only visiting Jamaica on the odd occasion. Bogle was an industrious man who treated the slaves, some would say, too kindly. His first child was with one of the black housemaids.

After working five years on the plantation, George's father bought an adjoining fifty acre plot and was soon grinding his canes at the factory. By the time one of the daughters of the absentee owner came out to the island to recover from a bad cold, he had the confidence to propose marriage which she promptly accepted on contemplating her chances back in London.

Her father gave a dowry of 150 acres, taking Bogle's property by then to 250 acres. They led a pleasant life except for the fact that she bore only daughters, his only son being George, born to the slave. As each daughter went off to school in England she decided not to return to the "dreadful Tropics". Only the eldest returned since she found no husband there.

When the landlord died, the great house, estate and factory all went to the Bogles through a series of purchases and bequest.

Bogle's son, whose freedom he had bought and released along with the boy's slave mother, was well cared for and also sent to school in England where he studied accounting and law. The daughter who returned, married the custos in an adjoining parish. When her parents died, as the legitimate offspring, she inherited the plantation with the great house and the factory which she later sold to her mulatto half brother.

For some years she had an overseer manage the estate on which operations were scaled down and some animals and slaves sold off.

When Emancipation came in 1838, the remaining slaves all moved into nearby free villages such as Clark's Town and Brown's Town, and the property decayed.

Bogle bequeath the 200 acres to his son who came out of sugar and began a line of rums. As the business flourished, he moved into Kingston from where he could better organise his exports. Later, as business boomed, he was to operate as an agent for British manufacturers.

He was a handsome young man and all the mulatto and quadroon girls were eager to please him. He settled with a dark haired mulatto girl and their first child showed no sign of blackness. The second, however, had a tan complexion and curly hair. The boys eventually took over their father's business but their families grew apart when the darker of the two married a copper coloured girl.

Because of the rift which had widened in the next generation, the darker Bogles sold some of their shares in the family business. This branch, from which Rudolph Bogle sprang, concentrated on the professions, producing great lawyers, doctors, journalists and social agitators and soldiers. Through the generations the men did yield to the social pressures to keep some "milk in the coffee" as did Ruddy's grandfather.

It was he who built the house now occupied

by Ruddy. He had been a doctor, a member of the Legislative Council and a shareholder in Bogle Industries as the family concern was now named.

As the family became influential and a part of the ruling class, they made a conscious effort to be strategically placed in all the important sectors of the society.

An uncle who loved playing polo was an army officer, another sat in the Legislative Council and his father sat on the board of several companies.

Ruddy was a problem child. When his brothers and cousins went to work in the business during the holidays from school, he wanted to go sailing. "Just like his uncle Robert," his grandfather would grumble.

Several times his mother had to be chauffeured into the country to the boarding school to persuade the principal not to expel him for smoking in the dorm, for threatening a teacher if he dared hit him, for being away from the dorm after lights out.

"I think you'll have to send Rudolph to get some army discipline," his grandfather told his parents when it was almost time for the boy to graduate from high school.

Surprisingly, his grades never fell and he came through in his junior and senior Cambridge exams. His parents sent him to travel in Europe for a year and when he returned, his grandfather called him, told him it was just a matter of time before the island got independence from Britain and left the Federation of the West Indies; the army would be expanding with the inclusion of an air wing; if things went right there would be an opening for him as a pilot so he should join up and get ready.

His grandfather knew the idea of flying aeroplanes would appeal to Ruddy. Weeks later Ruddy was undergoing basic training in the hills at New Castle before being sent off to Sandhurst Military Academy as an officer cadet.

The army did discipline him and gave him a sense of power even money had not instilled. He married an English girl in Britain and he saved a lot of money when he was commissioned since they lived in army quarters.

When his uncle Robert retired from the army, he had moved back to the house in St Ann and started a company to make a line of fruit preserves. Things were picking up as with the contacts established by Bogle Industries he had entered the export market.

Then a wave of pressure began. A youth group in the area began calling for the government to take over the 200 acre property and lease it to small landless farmers. The company in Kingston which supplied the glass containers said a shortage of foreign exchange prevented the importation of raw material. A trade union served notice that it was the bargaining agent for the 20 workers who were seeking 100 per cent pay increases.

The company recognised the union but suggested wage talks be deferred since business was uncertain and even a 10 per cent increase would mean laying off staff. The union called a sick out and then a strike when the company deducted the day's pay. Robert Bogle declared bankruptcy, paid off the workers, sold the property to Ruddy and moved to Miami.

Marc and Rosie were getting ready to leave.

"Ah want to share some of the fruits of my earth with you people," Ruddy said and sent one of the yard men to "get the stuff for Mr Fortesque and the lady."

The man returned with two shopping bags and he was followed by another man with a bag.

"Which o' the bags has in the pawpaw and mango," Bogle shouted to the first man.

"Dis one wid de writin' pon it sar," the man replied.

"We get him to love ackee and saltfish and rum but Ah can't get him to eat mango and pawpaw, yu know mi dear," Bogle said to Rosie.

"That stuff's too mushy," Marc said.

As they drove back into Kingston late that afternoon, the police had a speed trap and spot check at Ferry, on the Spanish Town Highway about a mile from the city limits. A policeman stepped onto the highway and signalled Marc to stop but as the car got closer the constable noticed the CD licence plate. He stepped out of the road and waved the car on. Marc smiled and waved to the constable as he drove by.

"I must say your police and soldiers have stood up well under the circumstances," Marc said to Rosie.

"I think that's one of the benefits of having the army and police under civilian control," the young lady said.

"Quite true," Marc said, thinking about the fifty pounds of compressed ganja he had in the bags in the car trunk.

That night while Marc was alone in his high rise apartment, he packed the weed into carton boxes marked "Confidential documents" addressed to someone in External Affairs, Ottawa. Chris Murphy was with him next day when he carried the boxes in the Chev to planeside at the Norman Manley International Airport.

7 DE RIDIM

Englishman a model inna shorts
Frenchman a model inna shorts
Capture wi hearts and thoughts
Bring wi inna dem ya parts.
An wi bidim, bidim
lik dem wid di ridim

So dat in 1838
Dem free wi through di gate
gi wi book an slate
but dat never seal fi wi fate.
For wi bidim, bidim
lick dem wid di ridim

Still bein alive
In 1865
Freedom spirit revive
for di system was a jive.
An wi bidim, bidim

lick dem wid di ridim

Well Bucky-massa slip
Economics tek a dip
But we never lose fi wi grip
fi mek Bucky-massa skip.
Yeah, wi bidim, bidim
wi lick im wid di ridim

Dat was 1938
A hundred year to the date
from di time wid di book an slate
an still wi never leave di gate.
Wi had to bidim, bidim
lick dem wid di ridim

Wi make to federate
Round bout '58
But it disintegrate
for some never tink it great
dat was bidim, bidim
Hooray fi di system

Still, in 1962
Massa say wi could go through
Dis is a true, true blue
It's freedom number two.
So wi bidim, bidim
wi move to di ridim

Well is [twenty-19] now
It seem bucky massa bow
But ... Blow wow!
Is im headman at the bow
So bidim, bidim

an lick im wid di ridim

Dem have Puerto Rican model inna shorts
Cuban model inna shorts
Dem say dem will bring spare parts
Lef wi wid wi hearts and thoughts.
But bidim, bidim
an check dem wid di ridim

For remember dis ya old time rule
A promise is comfort to a fool
words fi keep we cool
an use wi like some tool.
So bidim, bidim
scare dem wid di ridim
bidim, bidim, and check if wi fi rid im
bidim, bidim, bidim...

"What do you think about Cuba?" the dark skinned officer sitting behind the desk in the small room asked Clavel Smith.

"I don't know anything about Cuba, SIR!"

A stocky middle aged man in civilian clothes sat silently observing through his dark shades.

"Don't you hear that the Cubans want to take over Jamaica?"

"As far as I know that is political propaganda, SIR."

"In fact, it is CIA propaganda Private Smith," said the man in mufti as the officer studied a file on Smith.

"Smith, we have a mission for you. We believe someone is funding some Rastafarian groups to make trouble for the government. We're sending you to Cuba on a four week intensive course in intelligence gathering. On Captain Bogle's recommendation you are being promoted to the rank of lance corporal. You will proceed on leave for two weeks following which you will report to me for briefing before your departure. Any questions Smith?"

"No, SIR."

"Dismissed."

Lance Corporal Smith stood, stepped back and saluted stiffly and barked, "SIR!" then wheeled to the door.

"Oh, in the meantime Smith, grow a beard."

Smith straightened up from holding the door knob, "SIR!"

When Smith was gone, the little man began. "Thanks for your quick response Major."

"No problem sir, our first duty is to the country."

"I really think the Rasta problem might turn out to be the biggest one on our hands. They stir up an anti nationalist spirit with their back to Africa talk; they are capturing the entire youth population with music have you ever been to one of those dances and see how they carry on when they play those Bob Marley songs? And most important Major, they literally control the ganja industry.

"With all that money at their disposal they could spell trouble for the future of our country."

"Yes sir, we'll do our best."

Next morning Clavel left camp early for the

railway station. The old fashioned buildings and derelict cars on the tracks in the yard brought back boyhood memories. It was his first gateway into Kingston when he used to travel with his granny who sold provisions in the Coronation Market.

That was before the arthritis made it hard for her to hustle about. They used to board the train at the Mile Gully station on Thursday afternoons. He'd miss school that Friday. They used the train because it was the cheapest means of transport and it had cars especially for the goods of the scores of market people who travelled to Kingston.

When they got to the city, Mama would pay a push cart man to take the burlap bags of yams, sweet potatoes, dasheen and turnips up to the market about a quarter mile away in the seediest section of town. Clavel would wonder how she'd be so friendly to the man whom she had to pay a two shillings and six pence (twenty five cents) for his service, yet when they were on their way back home on the train Saturday evening she'd say "Mass Clavs, mi not taking you with me next week. You can't miss school too often because Ah don't want yu come up to push handcart."

Captain Bogle had no doubt about who should be ruling the country. Certainly not the dirty bunch of communists who had forced the backbone of the society, people like his family, to flee to Miami and Canada to start life all over again and to have to find jobs and live in apartments like ordinary people. Some of the "backbone", like himself, never realised until too late what was happening and did not send off their money to Cayman or Miami and now all they had was property, which, if sold could only bring in "the damn monopoly money".

"I should have listened to what Peter Solomon said."

"No man, these boys not communists," I said with my big mouth, "Besides no communist can't come to Jamaica, not over my dead body." Now the country is like another province of Cuba.

So Bogle had a plan. A scheme. He had quietly become active in the opposition party and he spoke to the party leader about the plan. Stir up a little trouble he suggested. It might even cost a few lives what's a few lives to save a country? but when Washington sees what's happening down here, we'll get some quick action; especially if it looks like it can spread to the rest of the Caribbean.

Bogle had never gone to party headquarters or to the leader of the opposition's office in parliament building. The fortunate thing was that they both had gone to the same boarding school so could legitimately meet by "accident" at old boy association meetings and since they also belonged to the same golf and country club, there were also those opportunities. But the meetings were never palsy and Bogle always acknowledged him with the respect due her majesty's loyal opposition leader from one of her loyal soldiers.

It was at a fund raising golf tournament

while slugging it out in the rough that Bogle broached the idea.

"Things gone bunkers around here. We might really have to get an uncle to get us back on the fairway," said Bogle.

"What, you don't think we have the right irons?" asked the party leader.

"We're a bit under par but if we can make the greens. I hear herb is good medicine."

He dropped the golfing pun and said: "If we can get something going to create a supply of greenback, I'm sure we can create enough fuss around here for Uncle Sam to leverage these pinkies."

"I'll have someone from the Canadian High Commission contact you. Invite you to one of those cocktail parties. Oh, and see if you can get your minister to look the other way."

"I have goat already. Who use ganja more than them damn Rastas. I going serve him an intelligence report after a few evenings of controlled terror. Nothing gets these pinkies to perk up like 'intelligence' and 'scientific'."

And so it was that that the network was knitted. Marc Fortesque called Captain Bogle with an invitation to a party and shortly thereafter, ganja in the possession of the Crown was being given diplomatic cover to North America. When Chris Murphy came to town, phase two of the plan was being written. After he got a taste of the honey he mentioned Brad Wisebaum and his friend Gunther Simon who had a small airline company in Barbados. Bogle thought Simon a great idea because if a time ever came when tips had to be made to the CIA, it could always be pointed out that the communist drug smuggling gun running plot had tentacles all over the Caribbean.

The plot would have gone quite well if the minister had not been titillated with the intelligence report about the Rastas and urged to send a man to Havana for training.

The Lance Corporal Smith in uniform bought a ticket for the diesel engined train. The 'diesel' was more expensive than the train. The ride was just as jolting but the diesel was cleaner and the seats were of fibreglass instead of wooden benches, attracting a more sophisticated traveller.

A loud horn blew and a man shouted "All aboard!" The train moved off "chug, chug, chug, chug" and he remembered Mama telling him the engine was saying "Bad conductor, good paymaster." As they chugged west, the shanty town of Back to with its rusty corrugated iron and cardboard hovels slid by, then there were green fields of sugar cane on either side.

Soon sellers appeared. "Pop corn and peppermint. Candy popcorn." "Peanuts. Salt an ital. Peanuts." One lugged a metal bucket, "Red Stripe and soda."

At Gregory Park, the first stop on the journey, the first preacher came on. He preached hell and damnation for the unrepentant sinner, raised a hymn and had the entire car except Clavel singing, "We shall have a grand time (up in heaven)". Although the preacher said a special word for the Lord to "guide an' protect our soljer and police" during prayers, Clavel was one of the few who did not give when the offering was taken.

The preacher disembarked at Spanish Town about six miles down the track and another boarded. Another service held, another offering collected before he alighted at Old Harbour. It was like a relay, as preachers boarded and detrained for the more than half dozen sub stations before Clavel got to Mile Gully, three haggard hours and fifty odd miles from Kingston.

Mile Gully was a one street hamlet with low buildings housing a few bars, shops, a post office, a community centre and several churches. Clavel caught a taxi with five other people stuffed in with the driver for a precipitous five mile drive up a bumpy, narrow, snaking mountain road to Maidstone.

Since everyone in the car knew him, he answered all kinds of questions on how he had been, how was life in Kingston and heard how it was good of him "to come look fi mama" and he should be "careful of dem gunman" when he got back to Kingston.

At Maidstone, with its strong red earth and smell of pimento, apart from a few distantly spaced houses there were two shops, a postal agency with tiny sub sub branch library and a primary school.

He had a beer with the boys in one of the shops and took jovial taunts about his single stripe on his right arm, before walking the two miles up to Medina which was really more a name on the map than a village.

Mama was surprised but glad to see him.

She had a pot on the fire in quick time and was tidying up the two little rooms while chattering away to "Mass Clavs". He brought her a bag of groceries from the shop at camp and she was happy for the canned sardines, sweetened condensed milk and rice which in these days were hard to come by in the local shops.

"Mass Clavs, Ah down on mi knees every night fi yu askin' de Lord to bless an' keep yu safe. When Ah hear 'bout all de shootin' in Town, an' Ah t'ink 'bout yu, mi belly bottom move."

"Don't worry mama, nutten not goin' to happen to me." He wanted to change the subject. "Yu get all the money order Ah send fo' yu?."

"Ah believe so mi son. Every fortnight, post mistress send one of dem boys to tell me she have something fo me. Ah don't know how to t'ank yu mi son. Gawd bless yu."

"Yu hear from dem in Inglan'?"

"No mi son. Not even a post card. Yu mother don't remember we at all."

"Mama, Ah get a promotion an' a goin' away fo' some trainin'."

She was happy because she assumed he was going away to England or America, one of the lands of opportunity.

"Praise de Lord mi son. So when yu leavin'? Yu mus' remember granny yu hear."

"Ah leavin' next weekend but is only for about a month or so." He was careful not to say where he was going. To Mama, Cuba was hell or worse. When Clavel was a boy and he misbehaved she would frighten him by saying,

"De blackheart man goin' come tek yu 'way to Cuba, so be a nice bwoy now." The preacher at church told stories about the godless Cuba where they took away children from their parents to indoctrinate them; how Fidel Castro made the children pray to God for sweets and when they got none he said "Pray to Castro," then when they did he gave them sweets.

Clavel spent some of his days further up the hills with his friend Danny. They were best friends since primary school days. Danny planted carrots and yams in the pockets of soil in the rocks around his house.

A footpath led to his wooden one room house a quarter mile from the paved road. He had no electricity and like the rest of the community, had no tapped water. Drinking supplies were stored in a drum which caught rain water from the roof. When the higglers from Kingston came to buy Danny's provisions, the foodstuff had to be brought out to the road on donkeys with hampers strung across their backs.

"Boy, Bredda Clavs, I man really gone into some serious farming. I man put a field o' collie up inna de woods because the food business alone can't work out," Danny said. He was matter of fact with the soldier since they had shared many secrets since boyhood.

He was dreadlocked unlike when Clavel saw him two years earlier.

"Yeah man, t'ings really rough," Clavel said, "because if me never live inna Camp, me couldn't pay rent inna de city. But Ah tell yu, it might be little better inna de country because at least a man will give yu a breadfruit, or a piece o' meat if him kill a goat."

"Ah true man, de country little better than town, and now a days since de people dem can't get de whole heap o' imported food, yu find dat more local food sell but de price..," he shook his head.

"Dat's why yu see now a one have to deal." He meant in herbs. "Is hard work still yu nuh, because yu have to out inna de woods all de time. Keep off birds when yu plant de seeds, keep on weeding de ground and yu see if yu want sensey, yu have to sleep out dey to make sure de plant den don't flower. An' yu have to have yu cutlass because man come raid yu midnight or early morning and yu don't even know how dem find yu field."

He sounded like an expert. Danny told Clavel how to cure the weed and how his main problem with storage was rats which seemed to love the stuff.

While they sat eating a bean stew that Danny had prepared, a little boy came running up the track to the house.

"Missa Danny," the boy in short pants said, "a white man an' a next man out de street askin' fi yu."

"What' kind o' car dem drive?" Danny asked.

"A white car like Mass U own."

"A'right, bring dem an' den go fi de donkey."

The boy ran back down the track and returned about 15 minutes later with Brad Wisebaum and Skully the taxi driver. They came to buy herb for Brad's friend Gunther Simon, who flew his plane in to Kingston from

Barbados, via Antigua and Puerto Rico en route to Florida.

Brad and Skully smoked samples of what they were buying and agreed it was worth the $30 a pound and took 100 pounds. They paid Danny $3,000 cash. They said that the only problem was to get the ganja loaded onto the plane at the Tinson Pen aerodrome. Gunther Simon, Brad's friend from his Vietnam days, had flown it there from Norman Manley International across the harbour, supposedly to be serviced, before flying to Montego Bay and then north through the Bahamas to Florida.

Danny suggested Clavel could help at the inland airport since he was a soldier. They offered him $800 for the service if he was willing and it dawned on him what he was doing for Captain Bogle when the officer sent him with packages to the airstrip.

He accepted the money feeling cheated and used by Bogle. Clavel hurried down to his grandmother's house and told her he was leaving immediately because he was getting a drive straight into Kingston from a friend of Danny's. She didn't like Danny's new friends because there were rumours in the community about what he was doing. Clavel could see Mama's spirit drop but he knew it would brighten eventually.

"Mi son give Mama a kiss before yu go." He leaned and she kissed his cheek. "Be careful Mass Clavs for 'Merica is just as bad as Jamaica."

It was a short briefing with the major. Lance Corporal Smith was to be in mufti by 1700 hours for transportation to the airport to depart by Cubana Airlines at 2000 hours for the Jose Marti International Airport. His suitcase should contain only civilian clothes. He would be met at Jose Marti by Cuban officials and a representative from the Jamaican embassy. There he would be further briefed. On his return to Jamaica, he should spend the first few days in a guest house while he sought alternative accommodation. He was given a contact telephone number and an address to which written reports could be taken.

The Cubana flight took off two hours after the scheduled eight o'clock departure. There were two announcements of delays before the boarding call for the prop plane. It was the first time Clavel was flying so he was timid as he sat in the cabin awaiting take off.

It was a full flight that had come all the way up from Guyana and when the plane was airborne he thought how the drone and seeming struggle of the engines reminded him of the omnibuses in Kingston as the drivers changed gear.

After a few minutes, one of the Spanish speaking stewardesses came to Clavel. She asked in heavily accented English if he wanted something to drink. Clavel said he would have a soft drink. She did not understand. He said soda pop and she asked, "Soda?" He said yes. She brought him a bottle of soda. He thought it was cream soda but it tasted awful. He gestured to her that that was not what he wanted. He asked for Coca Cola. "Cola?" she beamed and brought him a bottle of no name brand cola which tasted something like Coke.

Apart from the soda episode, the flight was uneventful.

They landed at the Jose Marti International airport a little past midnight. It seemed full of activity. A plane with strange lettering on the side was on the tarmac. Later he learned that it was a Russian commercial aircraft. An Air Canada and a Mexicana plane were on the ground. The man from the Jamaican embassy was dressed in dark trousers and light blue guayabera shirt jack like the little man who sat in the room when the major spoke to Clavel.

The roads to Havana were well lit and people were walking about or travelling by bus. Clavel noticed this because it was unlike Kingston where the city went to bed by seven in the evening. He noticed big billboards with pictures and words in Spanish. The only one he thought he could understand was one with the heads of four men against a red background with EL PARTIDO ES IMMORTAL in red on a white rectangular strip.

When the man from the embassy drove into Havana, Clavel was surprised how it resembled pictures he had seen of places like New York and other big cities. He slept at the Hotel National in the old French quarter and was picked up early next morning by the man from the embassy who took him shopping at the Diplomatic Store. The man advised Clavel to get things like soap, toothpaste and toilet paper as he might not be comfortable with what the Cubans had.

They went driving around the city. The man took him from west to east Havana driving on a road that went under the sea. He took Clavel back to Hotel National and told him he would be staying with Jamaicans for the two days before he went to the training institute.

That same evening they had a party at the embassy. It was attended by Jamaican students at Cuban universities and some 'brigadistas' who were supposed to be acquiring construction skills but who it was rumoured were being given military training.

"Last night the man come in?" one student asked.

"Yes," Clavel said.

"The man bring any mail or message?"

"No."

"So the man come through the party or government?"

"Through the government," Clavel said wondering how the fellow was so nosy.

"How long the man going be here?"

"About four weeks."

The student was glad. "Aah, so the man can take home some things fo' me then?" he half asked, half proposed.

Clavel was hesitant. "It depends."

"Is not anything much man; just some letters. The man can even post them when him reach JA. Letters take weeks to get through from up here man."

There weren't many women at the party except for one or two students. The brigadistas were all men and they drank Cuban rum and beer and became drunk. One of them was so drunk, he stretched out unconscious on one of the tables in the courtyard. A Cuban told the drunk's friends there was only one way of sobering him.

"Bring ice," the Cuban said. When it was brought in a small plastic bowl, the Cuban undid the unconscious man's pants and zipper and shoved a piece of ice under the drunk's brief. The man jumped up sober.

Clavel was to stay with the brigadistas two nights. After the party, two buses came for them. There were seats for everyone but two men fought over who should have the window seat. Clavel noticed that that was the first sign of disorder he had encountered since arriving in Cuba.

During his training, Clavel found that because of their indiscipline, Jamaicans were the least respected among the many nationalities that had come to Cuba for training. One brigadista had beaten up a Cuban man over the man's wife. Part of Clavel's training in the province outside Havana was to go among his Jamaican 'compañeros' on their 'volunteer' days into the fields to cut sugar cane and identify the main troublemakers.

8 GENESIS

"In the beginning
God..."
And then a
man
walked on the scene
"Let there be..."
a spotlight
The audience applauds
He bows
Vanity sits
behind a piano
and types

Clavel returned to Jamaica with a full beard, the first stage towards his new 'dread' appearance. He was convinced from his brief stay in Cuba that socialism offered hope for poor people. But he wasn't sure which of he local parties was socialist. What the government was doing didn't fit with what he saw in Cuba. On the other hand, the opposition party which was acknowledged as the party of big business, had pioneered housing and community projects similar to one he had seen in Matanzas, the province bordering Havana.

He booked into a guest house for two days then contacted his commanding officer by telephone. The major asked where he was and told him that a messenger would deliver his instructions which were to be destroyed after he read them.

A man on a motorcycle delivered the sealed envelope to the front desk. Clavel's instructions were to infiltrate the Rastafari Movemant Theocracy, get close to the leadership, find out if they were armed and their source of funding.

For the first time Clavel had doubts about his mission. He suddenly remembered his schooldays when one of the boys would irritate the teacher, possibly with some weird distracting sound: "Who did that?" Silence. "I said who made that sound?!" More silence. "All right, since nobody did it, everybody will stay in after school this afternoon!" If some little boy who was afraid of getting home late 'ratted' that would be a whipping for the offender but a black eye for the informer after classes were dismissed. At best he would suffer taunts from his classmates for weeks, "Tell, tell 'till yu belly swell."

Still, Clavel saw a positive side to spying on the RMT. He would get a chance to check out that beautiful girl he first saw in Southside.

The RMT meeting was being held at a member's place in the Hagley Park area near Half Way Tree. It was not hard to find because men, women and their children in red, gold and green knitted tams were on buses, in cars, on bikes, on foot, homing like egrets at dusk.

The meeting had started with the singing of the 'Ethiopian National Anthem' a tune from the Marcus Garvey Universal Negro Improvement Association during the period of the Italian invasion of the African nation: "Ethiopia the land of our fathers, The land where the gods love to be..."

Clavel had on a black woollen tam with a fine band of red, gold and green. While the anthem was being sung, a member told him to take it off as only the tri colour could be worn during its singing. Clavel meekly obeyed.

There was a big crowd choking the yard, overflowing onto the street. There were black people, white people. Rich people, poor people. Reggae stars, sports stars, university people, professional people. But most were poor people, including the president, Bro Sam, who it was said had the cure for the ills of the world.

It was the most organised and disciplined crowd of civilians Clavel had ever seen outside of official events and even then the police was usually on hand just in case.

The Bible reading was in progress. A tall man in a gown stood and said, "Psalms one." A hum ran through the crowd as those with Bibles flipped the leaves.

"Blessed is the man that walketh not in the

counsel of the ungodly, nor standeth in the way of sinners, nor sitteth in the seat of the scornful. But his delight is in the law of the Lord..."

A man shouted from far away, "JAH, RASTAFARI!" and the crowd responded, "SELASSIE I!"

"...the ungodly shall not stand in the judgement, nor sinners in the congregation of the righteous..."

VOICE: SELASSIE I

CROWD: RASTAFARI!

"...For the Lord knoweth the way of the righteous: but the way of the ungodly shall perish."

Clavel felt strange, as though they were reading the words for him. JAH RASTAFARI! the crowd shouted as the man finished reading.

Another man got up and read from Joshua, chapter two.

"Scofield Reference, Rahab and the spies," he said. He was reading from the Scofield Reference Bible.

"BU'N SPY NOW!!" a voice shouted.

"BLOOD FIRE SPY!" another voice shouted.

Clavel was nervous. Maybe something had leaked to these people. Maybe he was being set up.

But the crowd was only vocally violent and was patient as all the executive members read chapters from the Bible and then invited a member of the congregation to read. Then each executive addressed the crowd. Some spoke of history and prophecy. Some about the proof of the divinity of the emperor. Some, the conditions in 'Babylon'. An ordinary member was invited to speak and a visitor. Then the moment everyone was waiting for: the president who all the speakers had praised.

Bro. Sam got a rousing welcome when he stood. A shuffling began and there was a hum as those on the street pressed forward to enter the yard. The president started but the hum continued. An authoritative voice shouted "ONE VOICE!" and the buzz died.

The short, dark, greying man, whose age was hard to guess, spoke mainly about the army rebellion against the emperor and subsequent reports of his death and its significance in world affairs. He attributed the events to some biblical injunction that "judgement begins in the house of God".

He likened the events to the betrayal of Jesus. The president spoke about the members who had been sent to Ethiopia, who reported that the emperor was seen praying in an ancient church carved in the rocks in the mountains. He said that the RMT did not have to rely on the Western press to know what was really going on in Ethiopia. The crowd shouted "JAH LIVE!"

He criticised those who said Rastas should integrate into the Jamaican society and forget about repatriation to Africa and asked, "How can we give up a continent for an island?" There was thunderous applause as the crowd shouted, "No way!"

When the president finished, the business section of the meeting began. The treasurer tabulated all monies collected through dues, contributions from members and gate receipts from the celebration and dances. He reported how much was in the bank and asked the crowd for a total. They told him. Most tallied with the treasurer's figure but some were wrong. Then he enumerated the expenditures. 'Plane tickets for brethren to Ethiopia, gas for vehicles, food bill for the celebration. Again he asked the crowd for a total which he then told them to subtract from the first sum. The balance he explained was the amount the organisation now had.

Clavel was surprised and impressed. Not even in church had he seen such openness with money matters. He was in a dilemma and he had only just begun his assignment. Should he spy on and destroy these people who had no interest in local politics and who openly practised what they preached: the redemption of Africa and Africans at home and abroad?

He felt he would be betraying his grandmother even though she was not a Rastafarian. She was descended from slaves. She had told him how her grandmother was a child when slavery was abolished and how his great great grandmother was in a children's gang which had to weed 'bucky masa's' sugar estate. Somehow, the injustice was not as far away from him as he thought, because he actually knew someone alive who knew someone who was a slave.

Clavel thought also of having to betray the beautiful girl whom he had not seen tonight in the sea of red, gold and green but who he was sure was in the crowd somewhere. What had she said that day when he killed the gunman; "Save the gunshots for South Africa"?

Near the end of the meeting at about midnight, a speaker said those who wished to join the RMT should enrol their names at the table afterwards. Clavel enlisted.

9 TONIGHT

Tonight
a man thought of a woman and
spirit leapt
brainwaves crept across seas
thought was of slaves
and crowded hives of bees

Tonight
a man dreams
and it seems
not too much for sounds of mind
to seek out, find woman

Tonight
man thinks still
wonders when will woman see
across sea
when mind won't be blind

Tonight
man thinks of an age
a page of history
of love divided
love one sided.
she on an island
he on a rock

After Yvonne went back home, things were different between her and her parents. They didn't argue with her anymore about being Rasta or whether black people in Jamaica were Africans. The Stanleys treated their daughter with much more respect than before. The only rule they laid down when they saw other Rastas visiting, was that there was to be no ganja smoking on their premises. Yvonne enforced the rule to the letter.

She took Tafari out of the school in Rae Town and agreed to having him enrolled and paid for by her parents at St. Morris Prep, a school where most of the little boys and girls were taken and picked up in cars. The boy spent more time in the airy 1950s house of his grandparents than he did in the newer cottage in which his mother lived. He enjoyed reading the volumes of encyclopaedia with their colour plates and watching TV after he had convinced Mrs Stanley that he had done his homework.

One Sunday, Yvonne was having lunch with her parents in the house. Mrs Stanley had prepared the Jamaican Sunday staple of rice and peas, served with baked fish. She hadn't cooked chicken or beef because she knew Rastas didn't go for most meats. They were sitting at the big, dark mahogany table covered with a white tablecloth. The Stanleys knew that Yvonne was going to an RMT meeting that evening.

"Vonnie, if you had your licence you could take the car tonight because we hardly go out on a Sunday night," Mr Stanley said.

"Yes dear, why don't you get your licence? You can still drive, can't you?"

"Yes mama, Ah can still drive but Ah would need some practice before Ah could even think of going for the licence."

"I was thinking though, you know Yvonne, that maybe you'd need your own car. It seems to me that it's very difficult lugging about on a bus with the things you make."

"That's really true mama, but I couldn't afford a car right now."

"Your father and I could buy one for you..."

"Mama, Ah couldn't put you through that kind of expense. No."

"O.K. Vonnie, we buy the car, you pay us back like a loan."

"That sounds good, daddy. I'll think about it."

"And while you're thinking about it, get yuself a learner's licence and let's get you some practice."

They bought the car that same week. A Volkswagen Beetle. A few months later Yvonne was darting about in her yellow VW bug.

****

Clavel saw Yvonne at several Sunday meetings after the first one he attended. He did not get close to her because he thought it would be out of place to pursue a woman at such solemn meetings. Tonight, though, it was different. It was a dance, plain and simple. No speeches, no Bible readings, just reggae music all night. The hits were coming down. Bob Marley, Crazy Baldheads; Fredlocks, "Seven Miles of Black Star Liners"; Hugh Mundel, Africa Shall Be Free by 1983. Then the DJ put on the dub version of Bunny Wailer's Armageddon. The thumping bass was like an earthquake.

"Feel that weak heart, feel that," the DJ chanted, and, his voice like thunder, he rode the rhythm with the lyrics of an edited Psalm:

"Why do the heathen rage, and the people imagine a vain thing? The false kings of the Earth set themselves and the false rulers take counsel against the Lord God Jah Rastafari and against I an' I his anointed saying, Come let us break their bands asunder, and cast away their cords from us..."

The crowd was hopping and roared its approval.

"...He that sitteth in the heavens shall laugh: the Lord God Jah Rastafari shall have them in derision..."

JAH!! the crowd shouted and the black night air was electric. Clavel spotted Yvonne 'skanking' by some sisters and he edged that way. He stood skanking by himself and waited. When the next record started playing he went and asked her to dance.

"Can I ask de sister fo' a dance?" he asked leaning over with his hands behind him.

Yvonne looked up surprised and said yes when she recognised him as a new member. He started as if they were going to 'skank' apart from each other but she was offering herself to be held. If at first he was timid, now he was surprised. He thought he was being decent by trying not to embrace and 'rub a dub' to the tune like the non RMT members usually did. He timidly held her and she led off a waltz to the reggae beat.

She was well dressed in floral print dress and had the smell of roses. She wore a white, red, gold and green woollen knitted head tie which was interwoven with glistening gold thread.

"So you're a new member," she said. He thought she sounded so refined.

"Yeah, I man join at the Hagley Park meeting last year," he said making sure he sounded as Rasta as he could. He didn't want her to think he was a "weak heart".

"The man must try and live up yu nuh, because all eyes on the organisation now," (He winced.) "because the Pope and all the world leaders wouldn't mind if we could just disappear off the Earth." He calmed himself.

"True sister," he said. They danced in silence for a while then he said, "Oh, I man don't even have any manners. My name is Clavel Smith."

"I'm Yvonne Stanley," she said.

The record ended and they danced to the

next. Then he offered to buy her a drink. She said she was O.K. thanks. He thanked her for the dance and stepped off a few paces into the crowd. He danced by himself. She and the sisters chatted and danced by themselves. A record Yvonne loved started and she walked over to him and asked, "You want to dance?" He was bubbling inside. While they danced, a woman came up and said something to Yvonne. Yvonne said "Alright," and when the record ended she said, "Excuse me you hear brethren." He said, "O.K.," and she went through the crowd. He stood there hoping she would return but he never saw her again for the night.

Clavel next saw her at a shop run by the RMT, where members would stop by to pick up grocery items, sip a juice and talk. The shopkeeper was a longstanding member almost from the start of the organisation in 1970. But he was a Rasta long before. Since the days when Rastas were constantly beaten and their locks cut by the police.

He himself had never worn locks but he told anecdotes about the days of Howell one of the originators of the Rastafari doctrine and the commune at a place called Pinnacle; about Claudius Henry and Henry's son who was hanged for murder and attempting an armed rebellion in the late 1950s.

It was Bro. Ffrench, the shopkeeper who would educate Clavel about why the Rastafari movement started in West Kingston: how that area was where the African country people would congregate when they came into Kingston on the trains to sell in the markets and would set up roots when they came to settle in the city; how Rastafari, Revivalism, Pocomania and Kumina all dwelt side by side on the 'dungle' (dung hill) and how Rastafari the 'new wine' emerged as the front runner because it had a universal rather than parochial message of equality and freedom.

The shop on Wildman Street, had a front entrance where purchases were made. But the back of the shop was a courtyard with a few fruit trees and a paved area. That was where the brethren sat and reasoned.

It was an old Chinese grocery shop. The owners went to live in Miami. They couldn't take the fear of robbers and the hassle of chasing scarce goods to stock the shelves. To get rice, shopkeepers had to buy body lotion as well.

One of the sons of the owner was a member of the RMT and allowed the organisation to use part of the shop and he had his appliance repair business in the other section.

Yvonne pulled up before the shop in her car. Tafari was with her as they entered the shop.

"Greetings brethren. Bro. Ffrench, how yu keeping?"

"Wha' happenin' Sister Yvonne, long time no see."

"You go on man; nuh last week Ah was in here...Oh, hi brethren...Don't remind me...ahm...Cleve, right?"

"That's close. Clavel."

"Clavel Smith, right?"

"True," he said.

She bought a few items and was off again. "See you at meeting brethren."

Clavel said to Bro. Ffrench, "Nice daughter."

Ffrench said, "Very." Then he said "Yu have some very nice people inside RMT but some is t'ief and murderer." He paused and said, "Is Herbert Stanley niece," assuming that Clavel must have heard of the well known permanent secretary in a government ministry.

"Who's dat?" Clavel asked.

"The big government officer, man," Ffrench said. Clavel thought she was definitely out of his league and was sure that it was an accident that he had first seen her in the ghetto.

"Oh, so de yout' is her brother?" he asked wanting really to know if it was her son.

"No man, is her yout'." French paused. "But dem kill her 'king man'...de yout' father. Dem shoot him down Southside. Up to now nutten nuh come out of it." Clavel stiffened inside. It couldn't be the gunman he killed. That was just a teenager.

"A nice brethren," Ffrench said "Some man dress like soldier and police just shoot him down inside de house right before Sister Yvonne and the yout' one night. That's why de yout' dem must grow up to hate Babylon."

"Sister Yvonne must be strong," Clavel said. He was more relaxed. It was definitely not the man he killed in daylight. Someone came in to buy something.

After Ffrench served the customer, he said, "She is a decent daughter. Yu know how much o' dem village ram after her? But she chaste."

As she drove home, Yvonne thought how outstanding the brethren was with his reddish complexion, big beard and flourishing dreadlocks under the tam. She wondered how he never seemed to be raping her with his eyes as all the other brethren seemed to do. That curiosity is what gave Clavel his chance.

When the RMT held the next dance Clavel saw her a lot but tried not to pay too much attention. But she came upon him unawares and asked him to dance. She jokingly reminded him how she had left him standing the last time. The fact that she approached him was his gateway to paradise.

10 HAND WASHING

A doctor of medicine will tell
you that washing hands
is a ritual

For he learned from the witchdoctor
that this controls evil
spirits in sick people.

Dr Pontius Pilate knew his medicine well.

When old women were sacrificed
crisp on the altar of deception
he cleansed his hands
and washed psychic germs
which spread an epidemic among the people

And they cried
"The blood be upon our heads
and upon our children's."

They cried,
stamped heir feet with indignant penance
dug graves
and crowned the dead with golden wreaths.

Fire!
How many grannies burnt crisp?
Pilate washed his hands.
Arson?!
The Bible said grannies died to save Jamaica.

Truly, these were
the grannies of god.
Swiftly from the ash,
cinders and rubble
came a new Jerusalem for the aged.

The living had seen
the great light
That blackened their eventide into night.

The lady in the shop took Mr Hudson to the alms house two weeks before the fire. Even today it's still not clear how many men and women and children died in the blaze. Or how the fire started. Some people say it was deliberate. They say it was done by the CIA to show how wicked the socialists were. Some say it was done by the socialists to show how wicked the CIA were.

However the fire was set, going to the alms house was the final disgrace for Webster Hudson. He was born at about the turn of the century on a sugar estate. His father was the 'busha' or manager of the property. His mother was a maid. His father looked stately as he rode around the property on the big chestnut stallion.

Even though he was a busha, a mulatto with straight brown hair, the few local white girls would not allow him to court them. Busha's father had come from Britain as overseer of the same estate and he had a liking for the black women on the property. He got Webster's father and another son by two of the peasant girls.

Although Webster's father couldn't play the white field, he could lay any black woman. Even some of the married ones. The busha from Britain left his sons fifty acres of land and they did well with sugar on about 30 acres. The rest was not flat so they leased lots to the black peasants who planted corn and yams on the hillside.

Webster's maternal grandmother was one of the tenants on the land. So it was easy for her daughter to be laid by the mulatto landlord. It was even easier since the 18 year old girl worked in his house. Webster's father got frustrated with the tenants who often paid their rents with provision and the white women who ignored him. He sold out his portion to his brother and headed for Cuba. He left three children with three women.

Webster's uncle sold out Hudson Hall property and went to live in the adjoining parish and Webster hardly saw his uncle and his copper coloured wife after that.

Being one of the lightest complexioned

people in the district had its advantages for Webster. He was one of the few boys who never had to spend all his free time in the field with his parents because his mother and his grandma said, "No brown people don't dig groun' aroun' here an' you not no different. Yu mus' tek book learnin'. March Town nuh 'ave nutten to hoffer yu except yu goin' be teacher up a de school."

At school the teacher liked him, and to show it, Webster got more caning than anyone else. If teacher Campbell said, "Hudson, what are the lines of latitude that border the north and south frigid zones called?" and Webster said, "The Artic and the Antartic Circle sir," it would be a caning. "Bend over and remember this: ark-tic, A-R-C-T-I-C (whop whop). Antark-tic, A-N-T-A-R-C-T-I-C (whop whop)."

In sixth standard teacher Campbell made Webster a class monitor which the pupils pronounced 'man eater' and then a pupil teacher who assisted with the younger children and the duncer ones in the fifth grade. Webster sat and passed his First Jamaica Local Examinations but he never sat the second and third year exams because his mother couldn't afford to sponsor him further.

He wrote to his uncle in Westmoreland and his father in Santiago de Cuba asking for help. He didn't get a reply from his uncle but his father sent him a letter with an American dollar (four shillings in those days, 40 cents when the currency was changed to dollars and cents in 1969).

His father told him if he ever wanted to

come to Cuba, he would pay his passage and Webster could join his new family, because there was plenty of work there.

His mother sent him to an uncle in Kingston, who wasn't really an uncle but an in law of an in law, to learn a trade. Webster was apprenticed to a merchant tailor downtown Kingston who gave him six pence (five cents) a week when he felt like it. When Webster complained the tailor said, "Boy, better than you come in here to learn and had to sweep the floor as well and never complain. You have gold spoon in your mouth. Yu can either take it or leave it."

He took it and learned well. By the time he was 19, he was building suits for the Custos of Kingston and that set. Once an American staying at the Myrtle Bank Hotel on Harbour Street, invited him to come to the States and carry on his trade but Webster refused. He had a weakness for the Jamaican white rum and the Kingston girls.

Not a few nights he spent at a 'rags' dance at one of the many spots along East Queen Street before strolling with a girl to Breezy Castle beach or Victoria Pier.

In recent years when he went to the Bank of Jamaica to cash his ex serviceman's cheque, he would marvel at how the waterfront had changed. The Myrtle Bank had been demolished leaving only the tall royal palms that once lined its stately driveway; the market at the foot of King Street, beside the pier, was gone, land from the sea was reclaimed and a massive high rise hotel was now where the market stood. All around there were tall buildings such as he had only seen in Havana.

In Havana, because he had gone there at 20 to flee three young women who were pregnant for him, who would deliver in the same month. He came back to Jamaica with an even greater love for rum but in the five years he was away, the clients had drifted like the money he earned making suits in Cuba.

After months of doing nothing, he enlisted as a special constable. He was stationed at various locations across the island and as the saying goes, he spread joy among the young ladies.

Webster got married in 1938 and enlisted in the army reserves. It was the year of the worker uprisings on the waterfront and on the sugar estates.

Mrs Hudson was a dark skinned girl whose parents were teachers who only agreed to the marriage because they wanted to 'raise' the colour of their offspring.

The Hudsons had five children and she left him and went to live in England in the 1950s while he was working with the bauxite company in Manchester. She heard that he had got a son with a woman in the Mile Gully area. Mrs Hudson who was a nurse had no problem getting a job in London. She didn't know it but the boy's mother had also migrated to England to help clean up the mess after the war years. Mr Hudson never heard from his family.

He never recovered from the shock either because he left the job at the bauxite company and returned to Kingston. He went back to the house of the 'uncle' to whom his mother had at first sent him, who was by then in his eighties. Webster got a room in the back for which he paid no rent.

The uncle stipulated in his will that his heirs and successors should continue to provide this accommodation for Webster. Luckily, when the place was sold, the woman who bought it Miss Dorothy the shopkeeper liked the old man and let him stay. Besides, often he was her only company in the shop.

When the ghetto rebel war got so hot that she had to flee the Southside community as the area came to be called colloquially, she took the feeble Webster Hudson to the public poorhouse.

Rats roamed freely in the infirmary. They nibbled at the toes of the inmates. They ate an old woman's nose off clean. The place smelt like a septic tank and a morgue. Swarms of flies covered inmates who lay in filth and urine on their cots.

One night a man from an adjoining ghetto community entered the building and raped a crippled woman. The nurses and attendants did not realise she was pregnant until the baby was born while she was being fed canned sardines and the otahiti apples which some farmers used as hog food.

Mr Hudson was sitting at the edge of his cot in the dark, fretting as he had done every second since he was brought to the alms house. The night was fetid with mosquitoes and the stench of twenty other inmates who shared the twenty five by ten foot room on the ground floor of the wooden two storey building. He smelt smoke and was relieved that it would drown the stench even for a while.

"Maybe it will even run some of these damn mosquitoes," he mumbled. Then he continued talking to himself, "But the night really hot for May." The he heard wails and shouts of fire. As suddenly as he heard the shouts he saw the room become bright yellow and he was in hell. He thought to run but the idea remained that for a body which alcohol had weakened beyond its years. He stood and the wooden floor moved from beneath his feet. The floor of the room above and the beds and the embers and the smell of burning flesh and the taste of death was upon him.

Flames were licking in the sky from the huge bonfire of the row of buildings. The crackling of the fire competed with the screams of death and the hum of the voices of the hundreds of people who had gathered from the adjoining neighbourhoods. Sirens screamed as the fire brigade, police and soldiers rushed to fight the blaze and the crowd. The firemen had difficulty in extinguishing the fire because water pressure was low as a conservation measure.

Clavel stood in the crowd watching. His home, his undercover operating base was in one of the surrounding communities. He felt sick at the sight and smells.

The news media reported that all the political parties had been shocked and saddened by the fire. They wanted swift investigations and if there was any wrong doing, the guilty brought to justice.

The fire was condemned in Cuba as the work of the CIA and the leader of the opposition grieved for "some personal friends" at the alms house.

Queen Elizabeth of England and Queen Beatrix of the Netherlands sent their regrets. Mr Hudson's along with the ashes of the others got what amounted to a state funeral in a mass grave in the National Heroes Park.

****

Herbert Stanley was nothing like his brother. He was younger than Ken, had a lighter complexion and did not seem disposed to baldness. He had always been Yvonne's favourite uncle and she his favourite niece. She spent weekends at his house as a school girl and she and her cousins partied together. Uncle Bert really represented her first freedom from the oppression of home; the person she wished her father were. He never supported the idea of Yvonne becoming a Rasta but he never opposed it and his regard for her never wavered. Most of the toys Tafari had were from Uncle Bert whom Yvonne visited occasionally at his office or home.

He was a liberal. Believed in nothing. But when the government came to power he was pleased because he liked the rhetoric of empowering the poor and widening democracy from the grassroots up. He saw all this happening within the free market system and interpreted the use of the word socialism within the context of what obtained in Britain and Scandinavia. Fabianism. Social democracy. After all, he and some of these guys had gone to school together and he knew they weren't the devils their opponents portrayed them to be.

The Stanley's had traditionally been supporters of the ruling party, seen as representing the upwardly mobile black middle class and intellectuals. The opposition sprang from the labouring classes led by the brown skinned upper class.

But Herbert Stanley became cautious of the regime after more and more he had to follow the directive of the minister to appoint this and that young university graduate to head several new "units" to do special projects which he already had staff doing at half the pay. And then came the National Planning Council, meetings which he and all the other permanent secretaries had to attend and take directives and political guidance from party ideologues who headed the body. Even as a liberal he believed in the sanctity of the civil service from the political directorate.

Then in a private talk with his friend, the PS from security, he heard about the tapping of telephones and the spying on the Rastas.

"Can you imagine what they would do with my boy Ian if they start locking them up and torturing them to 'confess'?" asked the PS from security. "Since he left school, is just following company with this locks and damn silliness 'bout 'I an' I'. I trying to get him out the country, to school in Miami or something like that."

Herbert, concerned for his niece, asked for details and his colleague told him what he knew.

"Uncle Bert," said an obviously pleased Yvonne when she answered a knock on the door.

"How you keeping Vonnie," he said but she detected that he wasn't his usual jovial self.

"Fine thanks. And you?"

"So so."

"Come in Uncle. Ah just finishing up some cooking. You can have some of my ital stew."

"Yvonne, I have something important to discuss with you," he said not responding to the food offer. She heard the urgency in his voice.

"Sit down." He sat leaning forward at the edge of the little red leatherette sofa with arched mahogany arms. She sat in a matching one opposite him but they were close since she assumed a similar posture.

"You have to be careful," he said.

"I always careful Uncle."

"More than normal. I got some serious information from a friend. The organisation you join is under surveillance by the military..."

"But that is not news Uncle. Rasta always under persecution. We never have a dance that police and soldier don't come and interrupt."

"It's more serious than that. This is not just

harassment. They say that the organisation planning to overthrow the government and they have agents inside who telling them what is happening. On reflection Jerry's murder could be part of this activity I can't be sure

but I believe there will be more and people might be arrested."

"Jerry was in no plot Uncle. We don't want Jamaica. Africa is our destination. That is no secret."

"That's what the leaders of your organisation tell you?"

"Jah is our leader. The President is only an organiser. The president would never preach revolution. He always quote the bible, 'be wise as a serpent, harmless as doves'."

"You don't understand leaders, Yvonne. Leaders only want power. To rule. You might be too young to remember when Claudius Henry tricked all them people to sell their belongings and give him the money to take them back to Africa. The date past, all of them still here and Henry lived big after that."

"The President not dealing with politics. Rasta don't deal with politricks."

"The files show that he is supporting the opposition ... on their payroll. They say he's always talking against Cuba and Russia."

"Uncle Bert, who you believe conspire with Mengistu to overthrow His Majesty? When we deal with that is not no little local politics. We up against principalities and powers and wickedness in high places. Only God Almighty can stop all this but we play our little part."

"You may be right about the God part. But

you be careful. And remember what I said about leaders. The documents show that he really loves the sistren, even his brethren's wives," he smiled.

"Uncle Bert, you too rude. You really don't believe I could get caught up in that?" as they lightened up. "But the President is flesh and blood too you know."

"Whenever poor people try to free themself they always get a fight eh?" she said to her uncle as he stood and left.

****

Gunther Simon flew mainly missions ferrying business executives around the Eastern Caribbean or taking tourists on day trips to the Grenadines. But it really was the occasional trip from Venezuela to the US Virgin Islands to deliver packages of cocaine that made the business profitable. When his old buddy from Nam, Brad Wisebaum called about the possibility of a long term contract with government and diplomatic connections, he was cautious but pleased.

The contract with Caribbean International Services, ostensibly a consultancy registered in the Cayman Islands, made him both cautious and enthused. The continuity meant a steady income but the frequency increased the probability of detection. But what the heck, he had survived Vietnam with flak bursting all around.

He flew fortnightly missions from Seawell airport in Barbados taking Caribbean

International executive Mr Brad Wisebaum to various of its offices along the chain up to Kingston, on to Miami and then reversed the trip.

"Can't say I like the idea of working with a firm," said Brad on one trip from Miami as they touched down at the Tinson Pen airstrip in Kingston.

"Me neither," said Simon, "but it sure beats sittin' around waiting for work."

They alighted and were greeted by Marc Fortesque who had hired the consultancy services of Caribbean International on some development projects in the northern Caribbean. They unloaded several boxes from the plane onto Marc's car and drove out.

"You might not know it gentlemen but you are working in the service of democracy."

"Cut the shit," said Simon. "I heard a lot of that crap while I was dropping napalm on Geeks in the Mekong Delta."

"Touchy, touchy tonight," said Marc.

They drove in silence to the hotel in New Kingston where Wisebaum and Simon would overnight. Marc took the broken down M 16s, .357 Magnums and Uzis to his apartment and telephoned the Caribbean International vice president and opposition party general secretary that the goods for the firm had arrived. The goods that isssued random death in the campaign of controlled terror.

Before dawn he returned the flying duo to the aerodrome, just before a convoy drove in, headed by Captain Rudolph Bogle chauffeured by a private. Before Clavel was sent to Cuba he had driven the captain on a few of these missions but he was mystified about the cargo which was loaded onto the aircraft.

****

"But Yvonne, hear me nuh," he was saying.

"Jah know, Ah don't want to hear anything," she retorted angrily. "Just leave my blood fire house right now. Ah don't want to have nutten more to do with you Clavel Smith!"

"Yvonne, I man going leave de army an' try to..."

"That is none of my business right now. You, a Babylon soldier, use I to fight against Rastafari, and coming to tell me you going leave the army...Leave my house star. I tell you, if I had a gun right now, you dead...yeah man."

"Yvonne..."

"All them rumour 'bout the president out on the street, things that I and you talk 'bout...Leave star."

They had been in her bedroom. In her bed. The lights were dim and a Bob Marley tape was playing low.

"Can't educate us for no equal opportunity...

...The babylon system is a vampire

Suckin' de blood of the sufferer..."

They had just made love and were lying snugly. He was overcome by the love he felt for her although he was not sure that she wanted more than a sexual relationship. She had never accepted anything from him except maybe, a drink at a dance. In the ambience of the room and with the tune echoing in his head, a pang of guilt pricked Clavel.

"Yvonne, dere is something that I man want to tell de sister fo' a long time now."

"I thought you told me everything already?" she said coyly.

"Well not quite."

"So what is this now?"

"Bwoy, I man don't know how to say it," he breathed in deeply.

"You never short of words, not since I ask you for a dance that night."

He just blurted it out. "Yvonne, I man is a soldier. Intelligence officer.." Her spine froze. Her face felt hot and cold. She could say nothing because her tongue was heavy. She lay still and heard his story and then she jumped from the bed and trembling, tense she calmly said, "Leave my house Clavel Smith!" He tried to argue and she became angry.

He dressed quietly and she stood scared wrapped in her house dress, locks dangling, watching him like a dog watches its prey. He left and she slammed the door and bolted the three locks. She went to the bathroom, showered for about an hour and douched a dozen times trying to wash away their two years of love making.

Thoughts coursed her head like the colliding rapid streams of the Hope River in the hills over Kingston and they clapped just as loudly. It made her being feel pressured by some force like gravity or an electric current.

He had first seen her when she lived in Southside, she thought. The shooting...Who killed Jerry? Why had she gone to bed with this man? She felt suddenly as if she had betrayed Jerry. After his death she had pledged not to sleep with any other man unless they were married whether in a legal ceremony or in the same deep spiritual plane on which she and Jerry had become one. He (whoever he was) would never replace Jerry. In Zion ruled by Jah, man and woman would be Jerry and Yvonne.

Tafari had once asked her: "Mamma, Uncle Clavel, is he a real Rastaman or just a dreadlocks?" She had put the question down to boyish jealousy and not the childish innocence that usually detects a reciprocal innocence or lack of it in others. Tafari had said something about reddish locks not looking real. Now Yvonne recalled the talk and replaced 'real' with 'genuine'.

There was the nice brethren from New York who had shown an interest while on a visit to the island but Yvonne never felt the mourning period for Jerry had passed. Then there was Rocky who had said, "I man would be willing to provide security fo' de sister." Yvonne wrote him off because she thought he was too much of a brother having been close to Jerry and her for years; and besides, he had no locks so she felt she would be the dominant partner in such a relationship. Not that he was less Rasta but that he was less strong and might just be her bodyguard.

Then the President. He had approached her in the early days of her and Jerry joining the RMT, while she innocently danced with the

President at a party. She had told Jerry who responded that it took all types in the building of Jah's kingdom; that there were wolves in sheep's clothing. It was Jerry's pacifist nature. When two sistren had children for the President some brethren likened the leader to Solomon and David but Jerry told Yvonne that while Solomon, David and Moses were great men, his exemplar was His Imperial majesty who had one wife.

The extra curricular activity of the president was not known by many in the organisation but Yvonne had told

Clavel. It later appeared in a veiled story in a newspaper gossip column and Rastafari brethren from other organisations welcomed the chance to sling mud at RMT members and their President.

Why Clavel? She was a woman. He was a man.

Man, woman. Adam, Eve. The brethren always said 'Woman is the weaker vessel.' Eve. Beguiled by the Devil. Eve. Downfall of man. Yvonne. Beguiled by this devil. A rape of all she stood for. But this man Clavel would not stigmatise womanhood in the new Creation. He would give his life. She would repair the breach.

To Yvonne, the thoughts were in an instant but she realised that a rational process had occured. She awoke from the hysterics with a conclusion that these were the ways of man. But she had descended into a pit of hate for the personification of man: Clavel. The high tension was released.

She made up her mind. The organisation would not hear of this episode. Nobody would hear about Clavel's mission from her. Woman will be free when the Final Testament is written.

****

Controlled Terror was a successful venture up to a point. Uncle Sam didn't send troops to the rescue but the violence forced the government to call a general election. But the plan almost backfired. The Cuban DGI liaison officer in Kingston was as thorough as Fidel would have loved him to be. He did not just accept the request for assistance, send the man off for training and let matters rest at that.

When Clavel returned home, the Cuban comrade started an independent follow up of the trainee and the mission. His own intelligence on the Rastas showed that while there were 'progressive' elements, by and large it was a reactionary movement that was monarchist with many adherents so consumed by ganja, it was laughable to see them instigating a rebellion. His check on the Rastafari Movemant Theocracy came up clean even though the leadership was clearly anti government.

The comrade then turned his attention to the army officer who had recommended Clavel Smith's training. Information on Bogle was easy enough to get. There was a cadre of officers in the army, young men who had been encouraged by the local communist party to join the officer cadet training programme out of high school. After a few parties on the diplomatic circle, the Bogle Fortesque connection became obvious. He also noticed the old school and country club tie between Bogle and the opposition leader.

A little check up on Fortesque and Caribbean International suggested to the comrade a CIA front organisation. A few sleepless nights on Fortesque's tail landed the drug and gun running bingo.

He spoke to Havana about passing the intelligence onto the local government and after they completed their own checks, discovered a splendid chance to swap drug smuggling information with the United States for the right to buy restricted items from an offshore US company.

Having got what they wanted, Havana shared the information with Kingston, suggesting how it could be used to sink the opposition in a legitimate general election.

And so began an election campaign full of intrigue. First the government announced the resignation of certain high ranking army officers headed by Captain Ruddy Bogle. The official reason was that the army was being restructured to fit in with the economic resources of the country, notwithstanding the prevalence of terror in the society. The police force would be boosted to handle the situation as would the volunteer national guard which the opposition said was a communist type para military subversive force.

A week later, the government announced the discovery of a ruthless opposition plot to subvert the country with terror, aided no doubt, by the CIA. The Canadian High Commission was quietly asked to recall one of its officers, Marc Fortescue, who had collaborated with the plotters.

The general secretary of the opposition party and the President of the RMT were detained for treason and documents made public to show their involvement in subversion. Then the date for a general election was announced. Ruddy Bogle was declared a candidate for the opposition.

He made an impassioned entry to the campaign bandwagon. From the back of an open bed truck, which served as a platform at a street corner meeting, he displayed some theatrics to attract the crowd's attention. He shouted into the microphone that there was only one ranking on this stage tonight, punning on his army rank.

"Yes bossey, tell dem!" a section of the crowd responded, loving the aggressive display.

"...Look, this man fulling up people head with nonsense about freedom from imperialism, freedom to chart our own destiny," he said in reference to the prime minister. "This freedom put any food in yu belly?

"No boss." the crowd responded.

"Yu can take it to the supermarket and get anything?"

"No boss."

"As a matter of fact, there is nothing on the supermarket shelves anyway.

"I say get rid of him so that the people with money can be free to return and make the system start working again..."

The carnage that accompanied the campaign was blamed on communist attempts to subvert the constitution and CIA destabilisation. By the result of the election, the people seemed to have concluded that there was a communist threat. The business community had migrated and closed factories. There were no goods in the stores. Many children were on the streets begging and a new trade of cleaning car windscreens at traffic lights sprang up among them. People voted for a respite.

After the election, the new minister was purging the army of communists. The officer in charge of the intelligence unit issued an order for Clavel to come in. His former commanding officer, the major, had been offered the option of joining the disaster preparedness unit run by the new Ministry of the Interior or resigning his commission.

The names of the communists were supplied to the new minister by member of parliament Captain Ruddy Bogle.

"Smith, we have information that your real training in Cuba was to organise guerrillas in the hills to terrorise the country should a new government come to power..."

"Sir that is not..."

"Silence Smith and wait until it's your turn

to speak! You'll either co operate and provide us with the names and whereabouts of these terrorists in which case we may consider retaining you in the army, demoted to the rank of private or we can turn you loose and bring in every last one of you as corpses."

"Sir I didn't go to Cuba to train to be any terrorist. Major Bennett..."

"Major Bennett is no longer with the army."

In the little room painted blue, standing before the neutral polished desk behind which was the menacing officer, Clavel felt trapped.

"You'll have to murder me then sir," Clavel said. The officer glowered and said, "Dismissed, Smith!"

****

The youth in the area where Clavel lived liked him. They called him the 'red dread' and when they got to know him they shortened it to Reds. Many of them only went to school because "Reds say so", and gave them lunch money.

Some of the older ones who were out of school spent a lot of time at his gates because there was always a stick of herb and when there was one of the frequent power cuts he allowed them to play reggae music on his battery powered cassette deck. One day one of the youth who Clavel always urged to learn a skill and try to find work was despondent.

"Tell de man de truth yu nuh Reds, I man woulda juck down a bank right now."

"The man mus' cool Terrence," Reds said, "de beast them wouldn't make joke to just rip up the man."

"Yeah, but right now is like we dead already, because dem guys pon de hill nuh business wid we. De only time we see de MP or de councillor fi de area is when election time when dem come look vote an' hand out gun."

"A nuh joke," said a big youth with a squint who sat on the floor with his back against the wall.

"Is six o' we my old lady have yu nuh dred," Terrence said, "an' all my little bredda who pass him scholarship fi go high school...cho...most time 'im don't even have bus fare...Yu must see late an' absent pon 'im school report."

"A true man," the big youth said. "Bredda Reds, yu know nuff night I would go to bed hungry if de man man neva share 'im ital with I an' I?"

Since the night of the fire at the alms house, Clavel was thinking about organising the youth around him to take militant action. He remembered what Terrence had said. He thought about his own situation as a spy among the Rastas who he had come to respect. Now he was a man on the run.

He thought about Yvonne whom he had hurt. His atonement would be to help to improve the situation of black people. The president of the RMT had said that black people in the West could not be free until all Africa was free. Africa was being ravaged by famine and apartheid. Now even the President had gone to jail for trying to free black people and because of his, Clavel's workings.

Clavel thought the Rastas were not militant enough. They would never take decisive action. They would wait on Jah to do the job with lightning and thunder. He would support the African freedom fighters. He decided that a bank robbery might be a good idea after all.

He had a dismantled sub machine gun which the army had assigned him but the others would need weapons. After the confession to Yvonne and the episode with the new major, he was ready to take action.

Terrence and the big youth were at his house one day when Reds said, "Come with me for a drive to Gunboat beach."

They rode a bus from downtown to the eastern limits of the city on the road towards the international airport. Being mid week, the beach was deserted. Clavel told the two of his plan for the bank robbery and they were eager. He said nothing about sending money for African freedom fighters.

On another day they went downtown to Princess Street where it was crowded and sweltering with sidewalk sellers and buyers outside the haberdasheries and on the thoroughfare. There were several shells of burnt out or vandalised buildings left by owners who had either migrated or moved to the safer uptown plazas.

On foot patrol among the throngs was a young police constable in his grey tunic, navy blue pants with red seams carrying a .45 revolver that looked too big for him to handle on his waist.

Reds stood out of view inside one of the shells which still had its metal shutter but with a small access door open. The big youth stood outside propped against a column near the opening.

Terrence approached the constable in the human river that flowed in the middle of the street and in his best ghetto English said, "Hexcuse hofficer, you could come an' talk to dat yout' fo' me, sar," pointing to the big youth, "because 'im pick hup a t'ing off mi moder stall and won't pay fo' hit."

The officer, cap pulled down, raised his head to look over his nose to appear stern. If he could make an arrest now it would mean the end of his duty for the day on this horrid beat.

"Where de bwoy is?" he asked sternly. Terrence pointed at the big youth who seemed to get set to take off. "Don't run bwoy!" the constable shouted as he hustled through the crowd on to the piazza.

The youth pretended to submit and grabbed one of the constable's wrists just as Reds grabbed the other, and they dragged the officer off balance into the derelict building. Reds subdued him while Terrence took the service revolver.

They took off his trousers, underpants, boots and socks and walked out of the building casually through a back entrance onto an alley. The constable tried to stick his head out the opening to sound an alarm but with the cool breeze on his backside, he hesitated.

11 BOY SCOUTIN'

Blue
ebbing, edging at sore heels that seek
more than boy scouting
a postcard bay

Green
lining, reaching for skyline that beckons
winged visiting affluence

Read
these lines of love 'tween hills and sea
land and native son.

An elderly tourist in a turquoise beach coat which stuck one sided into the bottom of her floral bathing suit ambled gingerly across the sand. Her straw hat was drawn well down over her face. She stopped and looked across the small bay at the two boats resembling pirate ships flying red and white sails. One of the boats had just sailed across the bay where about twenty tourists were sunning on the beach in hazy sunlight.

Sailboats flitted by like butterflies and jet skis darted to and fro idly. Someone was floating on a yellow parasail against a background of banks of grey and white cumulus clouds.

The sea was navy blue in the distant horizon to the west, getting lighter towards the shore where it was emerald. Tall mahogany and almond trees shaded Folkestone Park.

A man walked across the beach peddling two large wooden carvings of Barbados and a hungry tourist group gathered around a man with a barbecue selling chicken and flying fish. Another seller walked by with a briefcase and approached a middle aged couple relaxing under a small almond tree.

"Want to look at some jewellery?" the hawker asked.

"Sure," the man sitting with his wife said. "What have you got?"

Resting his right knee on the sand, the seller balanced the case on his left thigh and while opening it said, "Oi got gold from Guyana and black coral."

The man pointed to a black coral pendant trimmed with gold and appended to a gold chain. "That looks good," he said. "How much is it?"

"One hundred and fifty dollars. Tha's only seventy five US," the seller said, handing the jewellery over for scrutiny.

"That'd be a good price if it were real gold," the woman mumbled to her husband.

"Tha' is genuine Guyana gold. Tha's a bargain man. You ain't goin' get a price loik dis nowhere else."

The woman looked at a pink necklace and said, "Oh, that's beautiful."

"Tha's coral man. Forty dollars, twenty US. Tha's a very good proice."

"We just came for a swim," the man said. "We didn't bring any cash but thanks for letting us look."

At that moment a big station wagon drove into the parking lot about twenty metres away. Four people got out. Two men and two women.

The swarthy Gunther Simon had driven the station wagon. He got out and opened the back. The hawker hurried towards them. He kept the case open and when he got up to them the women began taking up pieces of jewellery studying them. He carried the case and rested it in the open trunk. Gunther Simon and the women leaned over the case blocking it from view while the other man spoke to the hawker.

Gunther Simon lifted the bottom of the case and removed a wad of Barbados and US currency notes. In its place he put a new stock of a white powdery substance in small heat sealed plastic bags labelled 'Monosodium glutamate'. He replaced the bottom, raised up and paid the hawker for a coral necklace.

"I won't be around for about a week, Punka," Simon said to the hawker. "I have to do some business in Jamaica and Florida. While I'm off

Janine will be my banker." Janine smiled at Punka.

"Aw'roight," Punka said nodding and taking up his case. "Oi'll see yu then."

It was a call from Brad Wisebaum in Miami the week before Ruddy Bogle resigned that was taking Simon to Jamaica. Brad said this was a deal he couldn't refuse. He didn't give the details. All he said was that this trip would make enough that they both could retire.

The DEA man had come and sat by Brad while he had a beer at the Mango Tree in Montego Bay.

"Hi Brad," the man said.

"Hi," Brad replied.

"You seem to be busy as usual."

"Hey man, you sure you got the right guy?"

"Yeah. Brad Wisebaum. North East Second Avenue, Miami, Florida. Born in Wisconsin. Did Nam then came home and spent two years in California. I see you're with Caribbean International Services now."

"That's me all right," he said feeling as though something was about to climax.

"Well Brad, we've been monitoring your trips in and out of the States and we have a very interesting case made out against you. Dope, gun running, money laundering," he was enumerating on his fingers. "Let's see, the dope could be 10 years in the pen. The guns...let's say another three and..."

"Hey, I don't know what you're talking about bud, I come down here because I have this little cafe in Negril..."

"Cut the bull Brad. See that guy sitting over there?" he indicated with a tilt of his head. "Remember him?" Brad did. He had done a deal with the guy about a month before. "Jeezas!" he thought. The DEA man continued. "That's my partner and we've got everything on tape.

"Now Brad, let's say you help us to catch a bird flying in from Barbados." He mimicked flight by sailing his hand through the air. "Your friend Gunther is dumping dope all over them paradise islands but we want him in Florida.

"With a litle help from you, we could get you down to money laundering which'd be about a year in the pen which could be suspended depending on how cooperative you are?!"

Clavel had cut his dreadlocks before he went on the first bank robbery. He told himself that he didn't want innocent Rastas to be blamed for his action. The newspapers had a way of reporting 'a Rastafarian' held up or shot a man but they never said 'a Christian or 'a Muslim' if the theif didn't wear locks.

The STAR crime reporter's story said the hold up of the bank in Half Way Tree was a "lightning robbery executed with professionalism".

Clavel had to be stern with Terrence and the big youth. They wanted to spend recklessly. He filtered cash into the community through the youth who frequented his house. He made sure none of the new notes was spent to prevent them being traced to Jones Town. But the increased spending didn't attract police attention because it was near Christmas.

Although Clavel felt a certain degree of satisfaction in seeing the ghetto people happy, he couldn't help feeling that what he was doing was not much. Some people put new zinc sheets on their roofs. Some bought beds. A stove. Some invested in cigarettes and candy or other items for higglering. But the ideal of sending aid for the African freedom fighters disintegrated. How could he send the money? To whom? The Jamaican currency was being called 'monopoly money' since it had no value outside the island.

As he pondered on the next move he lit upon the ganja trade.

"Yeah," he mumbled to himself. "Is we from Jamaica suppose to control dat." He reflected on how much the man had paid him just to escort the herb to the aeroplane at Tinson Pen. "Yeah man," he said aloud to himself, thinking of the Yankee dollars. But how would e get into the states?

He took the train to Mile Gully. The police seldom ever stopped and searched a train as they often did the buses. He went by taxi up to Maidstone and walked to Medina. His grandmother was less active than before and she had not seen him in years. She thought he was still in the army because she still got money from him fortnightly.

Clavel went to see Danny in the woods.

"Bwoy, Danny, I man hot. You hear 'bout de half million dollar robbery? Me dat star."

"You juck down de bank?" Danny was

surprised. "I man tink de man still a soljer."

"No star. I man all 'knatty' dread but I man cut off through I nuh want Babylon say is Rasta do it."

"So wha' de man goin' do now?"

"Is dat why I come check de I Bro Danny. Yu remember dem white guy wha' I carry trough the herb fo' de time, dem still pon de scene?"

"Yeah man. As a matter of fac', I wonder how I nuh sight dem since dis month. Is 'bout dis time o' month dem usually pass through."

"I man woulda like fly out pon dem iron bird Ras."

"We can work pon dat star."

They were silent for a while then Clavel said, "Rasta, I an' I fi control 'erb runnings yu nuh star. Yu see when me go up Stateside, I man a go set it so dat I an' I control a portion. We can't make dem foreigner just control an' make all o' de profit Ras."

"A true man," said Danny.

There were two other big robberies the week Clavel did his job and in one of them a businessman was killed. The newspaper editorials were scathing. They wanted the government to come clean and say whether the nation was under the siege of terrorists or if the drug barons had decided that they were in charge. (It was strongly rumoured that the businessman was killed in a ganja feud.)

The newspaper wanted to know whether a statement by the commissioner of police could be interpreted to mean that acts of violence and robberies were being used to undermine the duly elected government of the country.

The Minister of the Interior issued a statement that the government would be issuing a statement after consultation with the top officers of the security forces.

The next day, the Minister of State in the ministry made an address to the nation on radio and television as the man responsible for national security.

The announcer said, "And now the Minister of State in the Ministry of the Interior, Senator the Honourable Rudolph Bogle."

"Over the past several days there has been a spate of shootings and robberies, which, understandably, has caused the nation great concern..." Bogle went on to enumerate the incidents and cited statistics to show that although there was an intensification in the incidence of specific crimes, there was not an increase in the actual numbers when compared to previous years.

He spoke of the possible links between drug traffickers and the increase in crime and said the government would not tolerate further assaults on the moral fabric of the society. Then he turned to the terrorist link. He said that during a police/military operation in Wareika Hills that very morning, a cache of ammunition, a home made shotgun, medical supplies, detonators for dynamite and communist literature were found.

Nobody was detained but the police were on the trail of terrorists trained in Cuba including a former member of the security forces. Finally he said that the nation should remain calm because the police were on top of the situation. In the Half Way Tree robbery they had already detained one man for questioning but his name could not be released for security reasons. (That was a lie to keep the people pacified.)

12 CELEBRATION

Mannequin in
animated motion
Mahogany skin
bewitching in
phosphorescent exposures.
Mannequin
inviting plunder in her gyrations
glazed eyes greened
by psychedelic strobe
Exciting spines with plastic tantalisations

Come wasp and see
the scorpion's sting!
Enter
you that languish and long.
Ejaculate you eyes
so filled with smoky want
Spill the wine of yearning
you who desire

and taste in your nostrils
the burnt carcass of your frenzied dreams.

The taxi dropped Yvonne at Clavel's gate. It was late and the street was empty. She tore a twenty dollar bill in two and gave the cabbie half and said, "Come back for me in an hour and collect the other half." He thought she was an uptown girl come to check out her rebel lover.

"De uptown guys too soft nuh?" he jibed her. She smiled and alighted from the car. She walked up to the door and rapped. Clavel grabbed hs gun and shouted, "Who is it."

"Yvonne," she said. He was surprised and glad. He chucked the gun and rushed to the door.

He let her in and said, "Ah can't believe it." He didn't believe that she would visit him after their last encounter. When he saw her hair and dress and make up he didn't believe that either. She was no Rasta queen.

"Can't believe what?" she asked.

"Dat is you. Ah mean, that you would ever come by me again. Ah mean..."

"You need to grow up Clavel Smith. You still don't know women." She was using middle class English.

"But the way how yu carry on and say you don't want to see me again..."

"Well here I am." She stopped the said, "Aren't you going to offer me a seat?"

"Yeah," he said remembering their little joke that he slept where he ate since he had no chair.

He smoothed the sheet. She sauntered over and propped her back against the head board and stretched one leg out on the bed and kept the other on the floor.

"Don't you have anything to smoke before we start?" she asked. He was elated.

"Yeah man," he enthused, "Ah bring back a nice smoke from Manchester just today."

He went searching for the herb then sat on the other side of the bed cutting it and removing the seeds. She said, "Do you believe in starting again?" With glee in his eyes he glanced up at her and said, "Yes." He did not understand.

"Call me Eve," she said. He thought it was a new love game. "Call me Adam," he said. He built two spliffs and was about to go for matches when she said, "It's O.K, I have a light. Come and get it."

She put her hand in her bag and held it there. He leaned towards her with a spliff in his mouth. She pulled the gun out and fired in his face. The silenced bullet threw his head back. She stood and emptied the gun on the limp body then she sat and waited for the taxi to return.

"Take me back to Le Club," she told the driver. When they arrived she said to him, "Can you keep a secret?" and handed him the other half of the twenty dollar bill and an envelope with more notes. "You never took anyone to Jones Town tonight," she said.

ABOUT THE AUTHOR

Mark Lee lives in the Greater Toronto Area of Ontario, Canada. His first payment for writing was as a 7-year-old in class 1A at Rollington Town Primary School, in Kingston, Jamaica. The class had gone on a trip to the Jamaica Scoiety for Prevention of Cruelty to Animals' hospital in western Kingston, and a children's radio programme host, Uncle Jim (James Verity) from Radio Jamaica and Rediffusion (RJR) was present for the occasion. He requested compositions about the trip from the class and Mark got the prize of 2 shillings and 6 pence (2/6). Somehow, as an adult, he ended up as a reporter/editor at all the major Jamaican and Caribbean news outlets, including RJR, and travelled in the region and parts of Latin America on assignments for the Caribbean News Agency (CANA). One trip resulted in his first book, a compilation of his reportage published as 'Life in the Caribbean Community – as reported by Mark Lee'. Southside Story, first published in 2000, is his first venture into fiction.